Brett seemed to be waiting, watching

"The Elizabeth Garrett Anderson is a children's ward," he said.

Her eyes flew to his face. Brett's expression was very set, very hard. He waited.

"Will is a child," he said finally. It wasn't a question, but a statement. Her world, teetering on the brink of collapse for so long, finally fell around her.

"Yes."

"Your child?"

"Yes."

"What about his father?"

She forced herself to try and meet his eyes levelly. Somewhere, sometime, she would have to tell him the truth about his son, but this was the wrong moment in every way.

"He..." Janey paused. Brett watched her. "Will and I live alone," she said, trying desperately to fight back the tears raging within.

CAROL GREGOR is married, with two children and works as a journalist. She lists her hobbies as "reading, first and foremost, followed by eating and drinking with friends, gardening and films. I am also a private pilot, but a lapsed one since becoming a mother!"

Books by Carol Gregor

Don't miss any of our special offers. Write to us at the following address for information on our newest releases.

Harlequin Reader Service
901 Fuhrmann Blvd., P.O. Box 1397, Buffalo, NY 14240
Canadian address: P.O. Box 603,
Fort Erie, Ont. L2A 5X3

CAROL GREGOR

marry in haste

Harlequin Books

TORONTO • NEW YORK • LONDON
AMSTERDAM • PARIS • SYDNEY • HAMBURG
STOCKHOLM • ATHENS • TOKYO • MILAN

Harlequin Presents first edition May 1988
ISBN 0-373-11074-X

Original hardcover edition published in 1987
by Mills & Boon Limited

CHAPTER ONE

'JANEY, Tom wants you in his office.'

Janey looked up, smiled fleetingly, then bent again to her typewriter.

'He says it's urgent.'

'He'll have to wait. It's only five minutes to deadline. Tom should know that. I'll go as soon as I've finished.'

The noise and bustle of the news room receded as she carefully composed her final paragraph. They had warned her that the new Chancellor was a cold fish, and it was true he had been hostile to the idea of a personal interview. But, as she did with all her subjects, she had charmed him with her warmth and sincerity, and when she had encouraged him to talk about his family she had finally managed to glimpse something of the private man behind the public office.

It was a good piece. She felt pleased with it as she dropped copies of it into the three trays ranged in front of the Features Editor.

She went to the cloakroom and rinsed the grime of carbon paper from her hands. With experienced efficiency she outlined her mouth with fresh lipstick and slicked perfume on her wrists. A comb through her hair, and a quick check of her outfit in front of the mirror completed the hasty freshen up. She swung her capacious red bag on to her shoulder and made her way back through the ranks of reporters' desks towards the Deputy Editor's office.

Almost every man in the room looked up as she passed. In her fashionable white flying suit, with her tiny waist clinched with a wide red and silver belt, she cut a dramatic and confident figure. But that was not all. She had stunning deep blue eyes, almost violet, fringed with thick, dark lashes, a pale and flawless skin, and a generous curving mouth whose ready smile made numerous hearts turn over.

She was known on the paper as the Flame-Haired Temptress, after her gorgeous tumble of auburn curls, but it was an affectionate, half-ironic nickname. Everyone knew that despite her head-turning beauty there was nothing and no one in Janey Goodheart's life except three-year-old Will and her work for the *Daily Standard*.

In turn, Janey, smiling here and there at the faces which looked up at her, sent up her familiar prayer of astonished thanks for having landed one of the most coveted jobs in Fleet Street.

She was one of the *Standard's* star writers, with a roving brief that covered every aspect of the news. One day she might be interviewing oil men on a North Sea rig, the next investigating the teenage drug scene.

The job carried the kind of salary that had lifted the day-to-day money worries of a single parent from her shoulders. And, as an extra bonus, it happened to be one of the few newspapers that was competitive without being totally cut-throat.

It was Tom Simpson, the Deputy Editor, who made this congenial atmosphere possible, Janey reflected as she tapped on his door. A blunt, no-nonsense Yorkshireman, he ran the paper's editorial staff with a fairness and open dealing that everyone respected.

'Come.'

He was standing at the window staring down into the hot city street below. She went across and looked down too. Black taxis crawled like shiny beetles through a shimmer of heat.

'You've finished that piece on the new boy at Number Eleven?'

She nodded. 'He was fairly monosyllabic at first, but he got going later. In fact, we ran over time. He said he'd be late for Cabinet.'

'Good piece?'

Janey gave a characteristic lift of her chin. 'I think so.'

'Good girl. I've got a corker for you now. Everything you could possibly ask for—not least a trip to the Western Isles, which I, for one, envy you from the bottom of my weekend sailor's heart.'

'Oh, come on, Tom,' she teased him. 'What about your sabbatical? Two months in Australia. This time next week you'll be heading towards the Barrier Reef without a thought in your head about us poor hacks toiling away here!'

He grinned in brief acknowledgement of the truth of what she said.

'Anyway, what's happening in the Western Isles?'

'Not what. Who.' He took a breath, relishing the

dramatic pause, the present he was about to bestow on her. 'Brett Britain. That's who.'

She stared at him, eyes wide, aghast.

'What?' She must have heard wrongly.

'Brett Britain.'

'No. You can't mean it!'

'I do.'

'No!'

It was a choking denial, a cry from the heart. Her legs were unsteady. Blindly she groped for the chair behind her.

Tom, shuffling papers on his desk, did not see her drained face and took her outburst for astonished delight.

'That's right,' he went on. 'Brett Britain. His first press interview since he hit the big time. The best-selling author that no one knows anything about—and *we've* got the option! Ah, here we are—his latest sales figures show he's outstripped everyone now. Arthur Haley, Jeffrey Archer . . .' Tom's voice was a blur in her ears. She felt sick, so sick that she feared her lunch would reappear messily on Tom's executive carpet. Her legs, body, everything, were shaking with shock. Abruptly she thrust her head down into her hands and felt cold sweat gloss the fingers that thrust up beneath her hair.

Dimly she was aware that Tom's voice had petered out.

'I can't do it, Tom,' she gasped. They were words she had never thought she would have to utter. 'Please. Put someone else on the job. Just this once.'

There was an ominous silence. She took a deep

breath, swallowing back nausea, and raised her face to his. It was greenish white, and her eyes, usually so dancing and alive, were dark with old ghosts.

Concern and curiosity flickered across Tom's face, but his tone was implacable.

'I can't do that, Janey. You see, he's laid down his own ground rules. It's you he wants to interview him. Or no one.'

Her lips parted in shock, then anger. 'He couldn't be so cruel!'

'He can—he has.' Tom frowned, puzzled.

Her eyes were big, searching Tom's face for some hint of reprieve. Her hands twisted in her lap, until, with a struggle, she found words.

'Tom, I can't. I really can't.' She swallowed. 'You see—no one knows this. No one in London.' She looked at the carpet. It was a horrible shade of lime green she noticed, irrelevently. Then the words came tumbling out. 'Brett is—was—my husband. We weren't together very long. It was a disaster, the whole thing. I haven't seen him since—I haven't seen him for years.'

The carpet began to blur and she bent her head to wipe away a brimming tear. Tom could be kindness itself, but he was also a tough newspaper executive, and Fleet Street was no place to show personal weakness.

How she hated Brett! She had thought he was out of the country, out of her life! She had fought to build a life out of the devastation of their marriage, and she had succeeded. Yet in a matter of mere moments that whole precious edifice was under threat.

'I'm sorry,' she got out, 'It's the shock.'

Tom waited until she managed to raise her head again. He was too much of an old professional to be surprised by anything. He went across to a table of drinks and splashed amber liquid into a tumbler.

'Now then,' he said, thrusting the whisky towards her. 'Tell me about it. Are you divorced?'

'No. It didn't seem to matter, either way.'

Brett had never contacted her since the day he had watched her walk away. And Janey had never paused to consider divorce, since the thought of remarriage had never entered her head.

'It wasn't much of a marriage. I was too young——'

'And it was all a long time ago?'

'Yes. Years.'

She laced and unlaced her fingers. Years in experience, if not in time. She hardly felt the same person any more as the nervous, passionate teenager who had chased Brett so impetuously to the strange and overwhelming city. In the years that had passed she had found strength in success, and maturity in being a mother. And treacherous passion had been firmly excised from her existence.

'And Will?' Tom asked.

'He's Brett's, of course. But——' a primitive instinct for protection made her bite her lips over her guilty secret, '——there's never been any real contact between them,' she went on eventually.

'I see.' Tom seemed to see too much for comfort. 'If it was all so long ago, Janey, would it be so terrible to have to see the man again? You've both got your own lives.'

She shook her head fiercely, setting her hair glinting in the sun that slanted into the room. The very idea chilled her heart. She had too much to lose, much too much.

And with Brett she had never managed to remain in control of anything—her thoughts, her words, her passions——She dare not risk the same thing happening again, but the only sure way of remaining whole and unharmed would be never to see him, never to speak to him again.

'I can't, Tom.'

Tom sighed. 'If it was a routine job, Janey, I'd let you off the hook. But it's not that easy——'

She looked at him with dawning horror.

'I'm sorry, lass, I really am, but you're being ordered to go. The *Standard* can't turn down a scoop like this, we've got the serial rights of his latest book hanging on it. No newspaper in the world would pass up such a chance.'

The last vestiges of colour drained from her face. Her eyes were a bruised purple in a shocked face.

'What are you saying?'

Tom look her straight in the eye. 'I'm saying you do the job, Janey—or you're fired.'

'Oh!'

A choking cry rose in her throat, but she bit it back, staring at Tom with horrified eyes. She was beaten and she knew it. Tears brimmed behind her eyes, but she blinked them back. There would be time for them later, in the privacy of her own room.

Tom sighed deeply. 'I'm sorry. But you'll be OK, you see. I've got a lot of faith in you, Janey.'

She shook her head. She wouldn't. She knew it. She could feel it in her bones.

'The man's not a monster, is he? He's not going to eat you for breakfast?'

She shook her head again, unsure of her voice. Breakfast with Brett. Through her mind flashed long-buried images, suddenly vivid. Newspapers sliding to the floor and coffee mugs abandoned as Brett reached for her and she slid luxuriously into his naked arms.

'No, he's not a monster.' Her voice, when it came, was thin and small. It was how she felt, tiny and vulnerable and threatened. She would only have to go within ten yards of Brett and she would lose everything she had struggled so hard to gain—her independence, her confidence and her peace of mind. Maybe even her son?

That thought was too terrible to bear! No! she cried out silently in her head. For Will's sake she would find the strength to match Brett's powerful presence.

'So you'll do it.'

She lifted her chin and with a deep breath managed to look levelly at Tom. 'You leave me no choice.'

'Treat it like any other job,' he advised. 'Be brisk, Janey, professional. Like you always are. Do the interview and then leave. You never know, it might even be for the best. You can't brush the past under the carpet. Much better to face up to it.'

'Much better it's six thousand miles away in California,' she said bitterly.

Brett's books had loomed at her from every bookshop and railway newstand. Never a day passed without him haunting her thoughts. But when she had read, on the gossip page of her own newspaper, that he had settled into a luxury beach house in Malibu, she had ceased to dread meeting him around every London corner.

Now he was at her shoulder again, a dark and infinitely disturbing presence, falling like a black shadow of doom across her carefully constructed life.

She took a deep breath, thankful at least that her tough job had taught her the strength and discipline to regain composure under impossible odds.

'Why can't I see him in London, at his publisher's office?'

'It seems he's spending the summer on Mull, writing another book. He's only prepared to go ahead with it if you travel up there to see him.'

'Why me, though?' There was deep bitterness in her tone. 'Arthur could have done it, easily. Or Joe.' She named the paper's Arts Editor, and one of his leading freelance writers.

'All I know is that the publishers said he stipulated the best—and that, he said, was you. That's why the *Standard's* got the option. If you worked on another paper, that's where the offer would go.'

She grimaced. 'There's more to it than that.' She was good at her job, but there were others who were equally good. Brett wanted to see her for some devious reason of his own, although what that could possibly be she had no idea.

Tom stood up. 'I'm afraid that's for the two of you to decide. I don't like doing this, Janey, but I know you understand why I have to. He wants you up there this week, so you'd better get planning.'

She stared blankly into the half-inch of whisky in her glass. It was at Brett's flat she had first tasted whisky, all those years ago. She had sipped cautiously at his glass, then shuddered like a child at the harsh taste in her mouth. Laughing, he had gently disengaged her fingers and reclaimed his drink from her two-handed grasp.

How far she had come from those days! Not that she liked whisky any better now, although she had learnt its value as an occasional useful medicine for nerves and shock. Just as she had learned to feel at home in the busy streets of London, and painstakingly learnt her craft as a journalist. And, even more painstakingly, learnt to find her feet as a mother.

At nineteen she had had a short cap of auburn curls and features that, although already stunning, had not quite lost the final vestiges of childhood roundness. Her wardrobe had been restricted to what her meagre salary and small home town could supply, and her knowledge of the world had been the sum of a few family holidays abroad and an avid reading of all the newspapers she could lay her hands on.

She had been eager, impulsive and demanding, determined to grasp life with both hands and ever ready to rush in where angels feared to tread.

That was how she had been when Brett had

known her, but she had changed. Oh, how she had changed! She raised her head with her chin set at a determined angle, swallowed down her drink, and with a nod at Tom left the room.

That was what she had to hang on to, she thought, as she made her way along the Strand. She had changed. She wasn't Brett's child bride any longer, and she wouldn't be swept away by the treacherous wild waves of passion and longing that had been her downfall before. She would face Brett as an equal, do her job, and go.

At least—she stood stock still and finally faced the deep and terrible fear that had lodged in her breast from the very first moment that Tom's news had sunk into her shocked mind—it would be, just as long as she guarded her words with care. Brett must not be allowed to break apart the peaceful, sheltered world she had so carefully built around herself and Will!

She walked on slowly, sunk in contemplation of what lay ahead, guilt pricking at her mind, as well as fear.

She had never intended to keep Will's existence a secret from Brett, but now it seemed the most vital thing in the world. At first she had feared that if she contacted him with news of her pregnancy he would try to insist she get rid of this unwelcome reminder of their brief liaison. Later, as Will thrived, it became harder and harder to write the letter which she was sure would land a furious Brett on her doorstep. Now, after years in which the bond between mother and son had grown stronger than anything she could have dreamt of, she felt she would fight tooth and nail with anyone who threatened this precious closeness.

Her thoughts made her uneasy, but she thrust away her doubts. She was terrified of seeing her life with Will broken apart, even more terrified of having Will somehow taken from her. Her fears were vague and unspecific, but they washed around her like an icy, threatening sea.

CHAPTER TWO

'ARE you all right, lassy?'

The ferryman noted Janey's wan face with concern as she edged her car off the boat and on to the island quayside.

'Yes, thank you.'

It was a lie. She felt awful. The drive had been longer than she could possibly have imagined, and she had felt as if she were driving, not north, but back, through old hurts and buried memories.

The long battle with her emotions had left her drained, and she dreaded meeting Brett.

Better to get it over and done with, she thought, as she noted the sign to the hotel where she had booked a room overnight. And instead of turning down the side road she set off straight away to find Brett's remote address.

All about her the sea was spangled with silver and the mountains rose clear and beautiful in the early morning light, their slopes covered with heather and bracken. She wound the window down and the pure fresh air was like wine.

But she was in no state to drink in the beauty that surrounded her. She drove through winding, narrow glens and along a lonely stretch of shore, following the instructions her secretary had handed her. This drive, too, seemed interminable, made tortuous by Mull's

convoluted geography. And to add to her problems
there seemed to be something wrong with her car. It
was pulling hard to the left and it became an
increasing struggle to wrench it round each bend in
the corkscrew road.

She swore to herself. This was the last thing she
needed, with her nerves already stretched to snap-
ping point! She pushed her hair back and edged
forward in her seat as blurred visions of granite-
strewn banks slipped past the obstinate car, her
irritation changing to anxious worry. She would have
to take the car to be seen to before she dared risk the
long drive home.

Then it was too late. A bend in the road proved
sharper than she realised. In vain she wrestled with
the stubborn wheel. It would not obey her instructions. Bushes and rocks loomed up as she gave a
startled cry. The car lurched, tipped, scraped against
a boulder and with a horrible drawn-out noise of
tearing metal came to rest crookedly in a ditch.

The shock froze her. Her head had bumped against
the steering wheel and now she did not seem able to
move from her seat. After the terrible noise of the
accident the sound of the nearby sea washed over her,
cold and remote.

'Oh!' A cry of pure exasperation shook her. What
price now her cool efficiency? Where was the aura of
competent professionalism with which she had
planned to armour herself against Brett? Slowly she
lowered her aching head on to the wheel and sobbed
with tiredness and shock.

'Well, this is a fine mess.' The door of the car was

being wrenched open. The voice penetrated to her like a shot of brandy. It was deep and resonant, and unbearably familiar. She had no idea if five minutes had gone by, or five hours. Swiftly she raised her head.

Their eyes met and in that moment the spinning earth stood still and her breath choked in her throat. It was like a thousand volts going through her. Nothing had changed. Janey realised it in an instant. Nothing at all.

Brett's gaze darkened as he looked at her. 'Are you hurt?' His voice was brusque.

She shook her head, 'I can't seem to move my foot. It's trapped.'

He leaned across her, feeling her ankle and foot. His touch, his closeness was too powerful. She closed her eyes against his probing fingers. He looked at her sharply. 'Does that hurt?' She shook her head.

'The brake pedal is bent,' he said. 'Can you wriggle out of your shoe?'

She did as he said. Then, unceremoniously, he put a hand under each armpit and hauled her out, standing her like a rag doll on the road.

'Lift your foot,' he ordered. She did dumbly as he commanded. 'Now move your leg, your foot, wriggle your toes. Good girl. Now the other one.'

She could think of nothing but his touch on her soft underarms.

'Now let me see your head.' One hand pushed back the fiery curls from her temples and gentle fingers pressed and felt her hairline.

Janey looked at him. She had thought she had remembered him in every disturbing detail, but nothing in her memory had recalled the sheer vibrant power of his presence. His eyes were darker than she remembered, grey shading to black, and far more penetrating. His mouth was more straight and sensual. She had remembered the square stubbornness of his chin, but not the shadowed cleft that emphasised it, or the fine lines of warmth and humour at the corners of his eyes. She had remembered his voice, but not how its deep resonance had made her glow and tremble inside. Nor had she remembered the husky male smell of his nearness, which now swept her senses with unbearable intensity.

He was looking at her, too, his hand still in her hair, his eyes going from her face down over the curves of her body. In the cool sea wind her silk shirt was flattened against her and the breeze tore at the ends of the scarf around her neck. His face was hard and masked of emotion.

'Let me go,' she said. 'I can stand on my own feet.'

'So I see', he said, with a cold irony, his glance taking in her expensive clothes and car. But to her relief he dropped his hands.

'You were lucky I came by,' he said. 'You could have been here for hours, days even. It's a lonely road.'

She took a breath. With distance between them again she found she could gather her scattered wits.

'I *was* coming to see you,' she reminded him coolly. 'I hope your presence doesn't mean my journey could have been wasted. I wouldn't have liked to drive for twelve hours only to find your house shuttered and barred.'

He laughed at the very notion of shutters and bars. 'If you must know, I've been up since dawn straightening the place up. I was on my way to buy some coffee for my guest. I thought our first meeting for four years could be a little civilised. Unfortunately on Mull that means a round trip of twenty-four miles. Had you managed to arrive intact you would have found my door open, the Aga burning and a note saying I would be back shortly.'

'You needn't have bothered. The interview shouldn't take long, and then I'll have to get straight back. I'll hardly have time to check for dust on the skirting boards.'

Brett looked pointedly across at her tilting car. 'I hardly think you'll be going straight anywhere,' he said. 'What on earth were you doing? Admiring our magnificent mountain views?'

'No, I wasn't!' she said tersely. 'There's something wrong with the car. The steering went. This is the first accident I've ever had.'

'The steering?' He looked back at her. 'That doesn't sound very healthy. And it looks to me as if you've wrecked your front axle pretty thoroughly. The only garage round here that deals with your type of car is at Oban. You'll have to get the car towed over on the ferry, and then new parts will have to be railed up from Glasgow or Edinburgh. And even then they're hardly the swiftest mechanics in the world ...'

'What do you mean?' Her voice was sharp with urgency. She had promised Will she would only be gone for two nights.

'I mean you can bank on the whole job taking a

good few days, maybe even a week. Time in these parts has rather a different meaning than it does in the metropolis. And no one will thank you for trying to hurry them up.'

'But I've got to get back—I've got commitments in London.'

He looked at her sharply. The wind was blowing his hair about, tugging at his jersey. She had thought at first that he hadn't changed, but now she could see there was a wildness about him, a gypsyish quality that had not been there before. His hair was longer and a shadow of beard darkened his chin. He looked like a man who had been living alone for a long time, at one with the mountains.

'Your office will understand.'

She opened her mouth to say that was not what she meant, but when she saw how closely he was watching her she stopped. She shivered inside at how near she had already come to straying on to the dangerous territory of her private life, but she battled to hold herself still and betray nothing of her feelings.

'Come on, you're cold.' Brett had seen the tremor. 'I'll get your shoes and your luggage.'

She watched him walk back to her car, a powerful figure whose every easy movement was imbued with unconscious grace. Already their meeting was proving much worse than she feared. Much, much worse. His attraction for her was magnetic, compulsive. It was an effort to tear her eyes from him. Yet as he returned from her car she forced herself to turn and survey the wild seascape.

'Get in. It's not far.'

She settled herself in the low black car whose seats smelled of comforting leather. Her own car spoke of a modicum of success, she thought, but this one exuded an aura of wealth and power.

Yet there was a comforting clutter of papers in the front and mud-splashed wellingtons and coats in the back. Oddly, she felt almost at ease as Brett sped surely along the twisting road.

Once or twice she sensed him glancing at her, but she steadfastly looked to the front until eventually he slowed and turned down a narrow bumping road, then came to stop at a grassy cliff terrace on which a white house stood foursquare to the sea.

All around them was one of the most magnificent panoramas she had ever seen. The house stood on a peninsula at the mouth of a loch. The sea in front of them shimmered in the morning light and small islands floated on it like dark mirages, a symphony in silver and black.

Brett killed the engine, but sat without moving for a moment or two. She glanced across at him, wondering why he made no move, and the thought crossed her mind that he was like a man drawing strength from what he saw. But she rapidly dismissed such a fanciful notion. It was she who needed the strength. Brett already had enough for ten men! 'What do you think of my view?' he said eventually.

'It's beautiful. I've never seen anything so stunning.'

'On a clear day you can see Fingal's Cave. And the white beaches of Iona. Unfortunately it's too hazy today.'

'It's still lovely.'

'Yes,' he acknowledged, turning to her, and as he looked at her a warmth softened his gaze until she felt colour creep to her cheeks and her heart squeezed of breath beneath her ribs. For a moment neither of them spoke. It was only a few seconds but it seemed like an eternity.

Then Brett said, 'I'm a very lucky man—in some ways, at any rate. Come on.' And she followed him to the house, disturbed by the intensity of the moment and puzzled by his curious remark.

He led the way into a warm, pine-panelled kitchen. She saw at a glance that it was the main room of the house, with chairs pulled up to the Aga and a huge pine trestle table running the length of the room. Papers and a typewriter were set out at one end. The sight gave her a pang. It was the same old portable that she remembered from his flat.

'I'll make you a drink. It'll have to be tea. You'd better have a dash of Highland whisky in it, too, for the shock.'

'Tea will be fine. And I don't need the whisky.'

Now the door was shut against the sea winds the room seemed almost too quiet, too cosy. Janey's nerves jumped at the strange familiarity of his closeness.

Brett saw it. His dark eyes seemed to miss little about her. 'Relax, Janey. I'm not going to throw you in a pot and boil you up for breakfast. Speaking of which, would you like some——'

She shook her head. The very thought of food made her ill. 'There's nothing wrong with me,' she said, managing to inject a note of crisp professionalism into her voice. 'I must phone the garage.'

'I'll do it, when I've made your tea. I've got some influence there. Meanwhile there's a cloakroom through there if you want to freshen up.'

She could see, in the mirror, that she needed it. Her hair was wild and her eyes were huge and apprehensive in a pale face. Make-up and a hairbrush did a little to repair the damage, but could not totally mask the edginess that was beginning to make her hands tremble.

Urgently she gripped the cold edge of the washbasin and regarded herself closely. 'Be brisk, Janey, professional. Like you always are. Do the interview and then leave.' Silently she repeated to herself Tom's advice.

It would be harder to leave with her car upended in a ditch, but she could at least hang on to the professional mask that had seen her through so many tough and gruelling assignments. She tipped her chin up and forced herself to relax so that the line of worry that darkened the clear skin between her eyes vanished. That was better. She allowed her fingers to uncurl from the basin's edge.

Brett in real life was more powerful and disturbing than her most magnetic memories, but he was only a man, she reminded herself fiercely, only another human being. That moment outside in the car had been deeply disturbing, but exchanged glances, no matter how heart-stopping, had no power to harm her, or deflect her from her course—provided, of course, she had the strength to handle them.

Back in the kitchen, outwardly poised, she sipped

gratefully at the hot tea and listened to Brett
telephoning in the hall. No doubt it was the accident
which had shaken her so badly, and now made the cup
rattle as she set the saucer down, but she couldn't
afford to let the shock throw her off schedule. She got
up and rummaged in her bag for her tape recorder.

'Brett Britain, July the twenty-second,' she said
into the microphone. 'Mull, Scotland. Testing, one,
two, three.' She played back the test words, then got
out her notebook and pen.

Brett came back in. He watched her from the
doorway. 'There really isn't any hurry,' he observed.
'You haven't asked what the garage said.'

'What did they say?' Her eyes flew to him.

'Their mechanic's away today. They can pull the
car in, but he won't be able to look at it until
tomorrow. That means a delay on ordering parts.
And they say there's some hold-up in Glasgow about
getting stuff railed up to Oban. The earliest they
predict it will be finished is Friday—and that's only if
it's not really serious. You might as well resign
yourself to a week's holiday in the Western Isles.'

'You're making it up!'

'Why on earth should I do that?'

'Then I'll have to leave the car. Go home by rail.'

'Oh, yes? And who's going to consult with the
garage? Pay the bill? Drive the car to London? I'm
afraid I've got far more important things to do with
my time than act as your motor manager. There's a
film script to be finished by August for a start.'

She looked at him mutinously, hating what he was
telling her, and inside her a well of panic was opening

up. Slowly she got up from her chair and walked away from him, staring out at the sea. She had promised Will she would only be gone for two nights. How could she break her word? And what if he got ill, or had an accident, with her marooned five hundred miles away? Janey's eyes widened with horror as her imagination ran riot, hearing emergency sirens and seeing Will's pale face searching for her in vain.

She took a steadying breath, but the scene in front of her eyes began to pulse and quiver. The long drive, the shock of the accident, the horror of the news he was now giving her whirled in her mind like a dervish of panic. She longed to turn to Brett and plead, 'You can't mean this—you've got to help—I have to get back——' but she held herself still and taut.

From a long way off she heard Brett say almost coaxingly, 'Surely it's not so terrible? You might even enjoy it.' She shook her head fiercely.

That was part of the trouble. She might enjoy it far too much. And if she did, what would it mean to her future with Will, the shell she had carefully built around the two of them? She could even lose him altogether, if some court decided to take a harsh view of the way she had treated his father——

While her body stood rigid and unmoving her thoughts blurred and loomed into fantastic fears.

Then there was a black roaring in her ears, a sickening lurch as the room wheeled and span before her eyes. She heard again the squeal of brakes, saw the ditch looming through her windscreen, and through that saw Will's pitiful arms reaching out towards her. She opened her mouth to cry out against the horror and as she did so her body, in final rebellion at the tension she had imposed on it, dropped to the floor like a stone.

CHAPTER THREE

SOMEWHERE from beyond the inky cotton wool that smothered Janey, Brett's voice seemed to be instructing and cajoling. She obeyed the deep commands without question.

It was his voice that had first struck her all those years ago, as she stood in the lobby of the local hotel, nervous and determined, hearing a sleepy 'Yes?' at the end of the telephone.

At that moment a prickle of premonition had chased fleetingly across her skin. She had a curious sense of future joy and pain, and an elusive certainty that life would never be the same again.

But she had had no time for such nonsense. She had a job to do, and one that was way out of her usual league as the newest reporter on the local *Gazette*. She was nervous about interviewing this up-and-coming writer, in town for a day or two on the film set of his first book, but she was determined to show she was up to it.

The news editor had heard that the writer was not enamoured of reporters and had given her the job simply and solely because she was the prettiest face in the news room, but his instructions had been quite explicit—six hundred words on Britain's life, loves and philosophy before he checked out.

She had nervously stammered out her request into

the phone, and he'd summoned her to his room, where she had been so flustered to find an apparently naked man sprawling carelessly among tangled sheets that it had been a few moments before she managed to focus on Brett Britain himself. When she did so she had found herself staring into a pair of grey, amused eyes. His look had been direct, overtly sensual, and his straight lips had curled into a smile of amusement at the situation. As he'd put up a hand to run it through his tousled hair she had seen taut muscles rippling under the tanned skin of his chest and shoulder.

'You catch me in a state of *deshabillé*. Miss——? His drawling voice told her he did not mind a bit.

'Goodheart. Janey Goodheart.'

'That's a pretty name—for a quite outrageously pretty girl. To what do I owe my good fortune to have such a creature in my room at this unearthly hour of the day? The local newspaper, if I've got it right.'

She flushed, uncertain how to handle his confident, bantering tones. Her chin lifted to hide her nerves.

'I'm sorry it's so early, but you don't seem to return telephone messages.'

'No, that's right. That's because I don't relish the thought of seeing my name misspelt and all my intimate thoughts misquoted in the pages of the local rag.'

Her flush deepened. 'I see you have a low opinion of journalists.'

'That's right.'

He levered himself slowly up in the bed, and she could see his tan was deep and even, and his physique was more fitting to a sportsman than a man of letters.

'But now I've seen this particular one I'm prepared to give her five minutes of my wit and wisdom.' His lips crooked in self-mocking humour, he indicated a chair. 'Fire away.'

'Oh no, you don't, Brett. You promised to get me to the station for the seven-thirty train this morning.'

Janey had whirled round. In the bathroom doorway stood a blonde girl. She turned back to Brett. A frown darkened on his forehead. For a second she glimpsed anger and impatience. Then he said to Janey abruptly, 'I'll see you tonight at seven. In the bar downstairs. Have your pencils sharpened.'

He was throwing the bedclothes back as he spoke. She glanced away, to the girl and to the scatter of female magazines and make-up that should have warned her he was not alone, and then she made as dignified an exit as she could manage.

He had been waiting for her that evening, and it had been marvellous. The interview flowed easily. One drink had led to another, and then another.

Eventually she had had to return to her office to write up her interview, and, working alone in a single pool of light among the other deserted typewriters, she had looked up to find him standing in front of her desk, hands pushed down into his jean pockets, the light shadowing his profile in sensuous detail.

No words had been spoken. Her hands had fallen from the keys. He had stepped round and raised her towards him, lifting her gently by the elbows. Then he had kissed her, and in that moment the world was gone and forgotten——

'I had to come,' he murmured huskily against her

ear. 'I couldn't put you out of my mind. Not your hair, your eyes, your lovely smile——'

Then he was kissing her again, cool, firm lips seeking hers, strong arms holding her close. Her lips lifted to his and parted against his expert assault. His embrace set her heart pounding as if it would burst and his hands, moulding her body to his, made her throb with urgent longing.

There had been nothing, nothing at all in her young life like the red hot furnace of emotions that clamoured inside her as his tongue explored her mouth and his fingers spread luxuriously in her hair. He made her feel as wild and wanton as a gypsy, careless of the past and heedless of the future. Wanting only him, his lips on hers, his body pressing close, all of him, in every way.

A door slamming downstairs had finally brought them back to reality. His breath was uneven and he crooked his mouth at her, almost rueful, although his dark eyes still held hers intently and his hands, linked behind her waist, kept her close to him.

'Who?' he asked.

'Mr Evans. The caretaker.' Her voice was breathy and shaking.

'Have you finished writing me up?'

'Almost.'

'Can I see?'

'It's not very good. There's never enough time——'

His outstretched hand was a command. She handed him the flimsy sheets of copy paper and sat trembling in her chair as he scanned through them. Although she did not know it, she did not take breath again until he had finished.

'It's newspaper tripe,' he pronounced eventually. 'But it's good newspaper tripe. Especially considering you've only known me for two hours and ten minutes.'

She managed a shaky grin. 'Mr Evans would never have believed that,' she ventured, 'if he'd interrupted us just now.'

Brett lodged himself on the corner of her desk.

'Write that final paragraph,' he ordered, 'and then come and have dinner with me.'

She looked at him startled. 'Your girlfriend——'

'I didn't notice you worrying about her a moment ago! But as it happens, she was never a very serious girlfriend anyway, and relations were finally broken off at seven-twenty this morning, when I put her on the train back to London. By that time I'd see you, you see. A vision of loveliness in my room at dawn!'

His tone was light, careless. It frightened her.

'Do you always——' she burst out. Then she bit back her words.

His eyes scrutinised hers, effortlessly reading her thoughts. 'Do I what? Break off one relationship as soon as I get tempted by another? Cast aside my girlfriends as readily as out-of-date newspapers?' He smiled at her, fully and enchantingly, showing white, even teeth. 'Do I always behave like a bounder, an absolute cad? I'm afraid, young Janey, the answer has always been yes—at least up till now.'

'Don't call me that,' she said sharply. 'I'm nineteen.'

His eyes roamed her face before he spoke. 'That's

very young,' he said gently. 'A whole decade younger than me.'

He stood up. 'If I were a magician,' he said, 'I'd even that gap out a bit. Make you a bit older and me a bit younger. But since I'm not——'

His voice tailed off as his eyes met hers again and when he spoke again his voice was low and serious. 'I won't be caddish with you, Janey. That's a promise. And all I'm suggesting is dinner. So why not type up, and then we can go? I took the liberty of booking a table at The Crown, just in case you said yes.'

Later she had no recollection of what they ate, but a vivid memory of all that had passed between them. She had felt both curiously at ease and yet breathlessly excited at the certain knowledge that some time later, those firm lips would claim hers again.

Conversation had flowed without a pause, although the gap of age and experience was evident. Brett had studied at Oxford travelled in the Far East, and lived in Australia. His career as a writer was finally taking off, and she was sure she was right when she had written, 'Brett Britain is a name soon to be on everyone's lips, whether they are book-lovers or not.'

Sometimes, as she spilled out her breathless thoughts and ambitions to him, she had seen a line darken between his brows, as if her teenage *naïveté* were an irritant to him. Then she had gone quiet, except for asking the occasional probing question that had him talking freely about his life again.

At the end of the meal, emboldened by the wine, she had said tentatively, 'You seem different now. Back there, in the office, you seemed very——' she searched for a word, 'flippant.'

He did not laugh as she feared he might. Instead he looked at her for a long moment.

'I'm always flippant,' he said slowly, his eyes searching hers, 'when I'm frightened.'

'Frightened?' Surprise darkened her eyes to violet.

'Yes, frightened.'

'What of?'

His look was so long and intent she felt as if a hand was squeezing her body of breath.

'Don't you know?' His voice was low, with a curious catch.

She shook her head.

'When I kissed you——' He stopped, took a breath. His fist hit the table lightly, in angry exasperation. 'It isn't always like that. In fact, it's never like that. Never before.'

She looked down, unable to bear the intensity of what their locked gazes were saying. He said brutally, 'I wanted to push you down on the floor and make love to you. Right there and then, without any of the niceties of courtship or seduction. I wanted it so much I was terrified of what I would do to you. My head felt as if it was exploding. No woman has ever done that to me before, I've always been the one in control. And that's the way I like it.' He took a savage swig from his glass. 'Unfortunately for me I'm not in the habit of raping virgins, especially not when their blue eyes are as full of shining innocence as a field of periwinkle. Not even when they behave in a most non-virginal manner.'

Her eyes met his again. So he had felt it, too! That

force of passion, powerful as a fast-running tide, pulling them down into violent currents of longing and wanting. She had feared it was only her own inexperience that had made her feel that way, but on another level she had known it wasn't. She ran her tongue round her lips in a vain attempt to moisten them.

'I——' she hesitated. 'I wanted it, too.'

'I know.'

His eyes roamed over her face and down to the thin cotton of her shirt. Beneath his gaze her body tautened and stiffened, wanting him again instantly, with the same brutal force of longing.

Embarrassed, Janey moved to conceal her body's treachery, but he smiled slightly at her gesture and she dropped her arms. What point was there in denying what they had both already acknowledged?

'Come on.' Brett clicked his fingers for the bill. 'I'll take you home.'

She stood by the car, sure that as he approached to unlock her door he would take her in his arms again. She longed for that moment. Without his enfolding embrace she felt naked and incomplete. But he only ushered her in brusquely.

Outside her father's house he killed the engine. Janey turned eagerly towards him, but he had withdrawn from her, was holding himself firmly back.

'Thank you for dinner,' she said flatly, 'and for the interview.'

'That's a nice house,' Brett said eventually.

'It is,' she acknowledged, 'although the garden is

running wild. Daddy's a doctor, and he never seems to have any time to himself. And his health isn't good, so he can't tackle the heavy work.'

Brett said, oddly, 'I'd like to have met him—and your mother.'

She'd turned startled eyes to his. 'My mother's dead. She died nine years ago.'

'Oh, I'm sorry. But maybe I'll meet your father one day—you never know.'

'It's hardly likely. You leave on Friday, and there's nothing to bring you back here. It isn't even on the way to anywhere—unless you're taking the branch line to Banbury.' There was bitterness in her tone, and her heart sank further as he acknowledged the truth of her words.

Then he was out of the car, helping her out. 'In you go—we've both got work to do tomorrow.'

'Brett——' Her face was upturned to him.

'Janey—please. For both our sakes.'

She stood without moving, only knowing that with every nerve in her body she ached for him to kiss her again. In the darkness he was a powerful silhouette next to her. Then, after a long silence, he put out a hand and lightly touched her neck below her ear. Slowly his fingers trailed down, softly tracing her slender neck, the hollows of her throat. Janey shivered, shot through with the yearning desire that sprang to life at his merest touch. Lightly he moulded her shoulders with each hand, then his hands were slipped round her back, pulling her closer until she felt his breath on her cheek. His lips touched hers, gently at first, tenderly exploring the softness of her wide mouth, moving to kiss her cheeks and neck, then back to claim her lips again. His embrace hardened as she yielded instantly, opening her mouth to the possession of his, as his tongue roamed the softness, knowing her and taking her.

He groaned as she arched against him and their bodies met, length to length, and his hands moved more roughly, more urgently, slipping under her jacket to mould her back, and then sliding round to shape each young full breast.

She shook under his touch, throbbing deep inside, as the soft curves swelled into his hands and her lips met the growing passion of his.

Her breath seemed taken from her. She was liquid fire, molten longing, wanting all of him, pressing herself against his urgent, desiring body.

'Janey,' he groaned warningly, but she kissed him harder until his hand moved to part the buttons of her shirt. She shuddered as his fingers touched the warm flesh, and threw her head back as he unclipped the flimsy lace and her breasts tumbled free, naked to his caresses.

His hands took each one, wonderingly, yet firmly. Then his head bent to kiss and rouse each hardened nipple.

'Oh!' It was exquisite pleasure, almost pain, setting her body throbbing for him until her hands, of their own accord, were running over his back and pulling his hips closer against her. She hardly knew what she was doing as her fingers felt the rough texture of his jeans and sought the buckle of his belt.

As she did so, Brett tore his mouth from her body,

and buried his head against her hair, his breath rasping and hard.

'I won't do it,' he ground out, as if to himself.

She pulled him close, her breasts pressing against his shirt, her body still moving against his.

'No!' He pulled back from her, his head turned from her.

He took a breath, then turned back, his eyes looking down at her naked beauty, the disarray of her dress.

Janey felt no embarrassment under his gaze, only a tumult of confused emotions, and she stood without moving as, sighing deeply, he restored her dress to order. She watched him as he did up the tiny buttons with rough gentleness.

'Why?' she asked him shakily.

'Because you're too young, too innocent—and anyway, this is hardly the time or place,' he added harshly.

But she shook her head impatiently. 'No. I don't mean that. I know that. I mean, why is it like this for us? You could do anything with me, anything at all—and yesterday I didn't even know you.'

He crooked his mouth at her tone and put out a hand to stroke a wisp of curl from her cheek.

'Sweet Janey, I don't think you're a wanton hussy, if that's what you mean.' The black depths of his eyes searched her face, slowly and intently, replacing the dying throb of desire with a piercing sweet longing to know him and care for him, this stranger who had come so abruptly into her life.

And then—quite suddenly—she realised what he meant when he had told her, earlier, that he was frightened. Not just the raw, heedless passion that ignited between them at every touch, but something much older, much deeper, that lay behind it.

Somewhere in her head the words 'my man' took shape and sound. She wanted to claim Brett as her own in mind, body and spirit, and she guessed that he, too, felt ripples of this ancient cleaving.

That was what he was frightened of. Not her youth, not her innocence, but the commitment that it threatened—the deep bonding of souls that could bind a person for a lifetime. All this passed through her mind in a flash, but even as she sorted out her wild thoughts, he was pushing her gently up the weed-strewn drive.

'Goodnight, Janey, my love. Sweet dreams.'

And he was gone, as she thought, for ever.

CHAPTER FOUR

But Janey's dreams weren't sweet, not that night, nor for many afterwards. 'No,' she protested wretchedly, as she felt Brett's hands push her away again, out of his life. 'No, no!' She turned her face into the pillow, seeking solace for her loss, but she was alone and there was no Brett to hold her close. His hands at her shoulders had pushed her away. He hadn't wanted her, not then, and not later.

'Janey, it's all right. It's only a dream.'

Slowly she struggled up through layer after layer of oblivion. There were hands at her shoulders, but they were easing her back against the pillows.

'Easy,' said Brett.

He stood over her, a dark figure, his grasp restraining her until he felt her relax out of the nightmare.

She felt so confused that at first there was no surprise in seeing him bending over her. Then she remembered, and sat up in bed with a start. She was wearing only her pants and a loose white T-shirt that must be his.

'I didn't think you'd want those expensive designer clothes of yours ruined in bed,' he said.

'You undressed me?'

He made a pantomime of looking around.

'Well, there's no one else here. My extensive staff must have taken the day off. And if someone faints

41

you have to remove all restrictive clothing—it's a basic rule of first aid. Anyway, not to put too fine a point on it, I've seen it all before.'

She flushed angrily, and watched in silence as he moved to draw back the curtains. Framed in the window was the same lovely pattern of islands, only now the view was flooded with the low, ripe sunshine of early evening.

'The master bedroom,' he observed. 'With one of the finest views in the country. You can lie in bed and take it all in without even lifting your head from the pillow.'

She looked around, still dull and slow-witted. Like the downstairs kitchen, the room was snugly pine-clad. There was a man's watch on the bedside table, and a pile of books.

'It's your room.'

'It happened to have the only bed that was made up when you staged your dramatic fainting act.'

'What's the time?'

'Past six. You must have been exhausted. You slept all day. I looked in from time to time, but you were dead to the world.' He scrutinised her face closely. 'In fact it looked to me as if you were sleeping off weeks and months of exhaustion, not one night's missed sleep. I only woke you now because your dreams didn't seem to be giving you much pleasure.'

Janey leant back on the pillows. It was true she had a peculiar and entirely misplaced sense of well-being. She felt rested and warm and safe in this remote Highland house, just as she had fleetingly felt at ease when Brett had sped her home here. She would have liked the moment to be held suspended in time. But responsibilities were already crowding her mind.

'I must phone people and tell them what's happened.'

'I'll ring your office, if you like.'

'No. I don't mean the office——' She stopped abruptly, caught his eye and looked quickly away. 'I——' she faltered, searching her sleep-fogged brain for some acceptable half-truth. 'I share a house with friends. I must tell them I won't be back when they expect me.'

It was a version of the truth, albeit an edited one. One of the many strokes of good fortune in her recent life had been the chance to buy the basement flat in the rambling family home of John Pardow, the *Standard*'s Sports Editor, and his wife, Ann. Their young family had quickly become Will's second home, and she knew he was always in safe hands when she went away.

His eyes bored into her, disbelieving. 'I see. It must be a very friendly house, if it's so important to tell these friends your every move.'

She tipped her chin defiantly, 'It is.' She flung the covers back with an angry gesture. She had no need to explain anything to him. The T-shirt barely came to the top of her slim legs, but she didn't care. 'Can I use your phone?'

'Of course. It's in the hall at the bottom of the stairs.'

Where he would hear every word, she thought.

'Thank you.'

On legs that were surprisingly shaky she hurried down the stairs. She felt strange and unreal, as if she had just suffered a short and violent dose of flu.

'Ann?'

'Janey, hello. How's it going?'

'Look—something's happened. I had an accident. I'm all right, but the car's a mess. I won't be able to get back for a few days.'

'Oh, Janey, are you sure you're OK?'

'Yes, I'm fine. I'm just worried about——' She stopped. 'It's difficult to talk, I can't really explain. But will you try and explain what's happened? I promise I'll be home as soon as I can. And I'll ring you again soon.'

'But don't you want to tell Will yourself? He's here. He's just had his bath.'

'No, I can't! I'll tell you why when I get back. Just give him my love, will you?'

'Of course.' Ann sounded puzzled. 'And don't worry. He'll be fine here with us. He understands you have to go away sometimes. But you sound odd, Janey. You make sure you look after yourself, you hear?'

'Yes, I will. Thank you. I don't know what I'd do without you.'

Her legs were even shakier as she remounted the stairs. Brett still waited in the bedroom.

'All right?' he asked.

She nodded, unable to trust her voice. There was a lump in her throat as she thought of how she had had to refuse to speak to her son.

'Now get back into bed. You've had a nasty shock. And drink this—best Highland malt.' He handed her a glass and she climbed back beneath the sheets. She had planned to ask him to drive her to her hotel, but she was suddenly all too glad to relinquish any effort until tomorrow.

She drank the whisky, looking at him guardedly over the edge of the glass. Brett sat on the side of the bed and watched her. Neither of them spoke and the room seemed to vibrate with unvoiced thoughts.

After a time he put out a hand and moved a lock of her hair.

'Does that hurt?' He touched a bruise on her forehead lightly with a thumb.

She reared back instinctively from his touch and his eyes darkened as he dropped his hand.

'I think you'll live. You've been lucky.'

'I would have been luckier still if I hadn't come up here in the first place,' she said bitterly. That light stroke of his hand had been infinitely disturbing.

His mouth set, etching stubborn lines on the lean planes of his cheeks. 'It's your job to go where you're sent. You ought to be used to it by now.'

'And you made sure I was sent here!'

'I've got an important deadline to meet. I need to work at full stretch for the next few weeks. I don't have time for pleasure jaunts to London.'

'So everyone else just has to fit in with your plans! I don't suppose it crossed your mind that it might not be convenient for other people?'

'I'm afraid, to put it bluntly, I'm the hot property in this deal. It's a seller's market, and I'm the one doing the selling. If you, or your newspaper had wanted to turn me down, they could have done.'

'You know it doesn't work like that! But I suppose you've got so used to calling the shots now that you've forgotten what ordinary human courtesies are all about!'

She shook her head angrily and the T-shirt slipped

loose from one shoulder. She hitched it back carelessly, glaring at him with the freezing stare that had sent so many would-be suitors packing. 'And why me, anyway?'

Brett hesitated, pushed a hand through his hair. 'What did the paper tell you?' he parried.

'They said you'd stipulated the best, and that was me. It's very flattering, but it just doesn't ring true. I'm good—but so are plenty of others. You could have chosen Mike Aspen, for a start. He's a friend of yours, isn't he?'

'Well done. You've been doing your homework. I like Mike, but I don't happen to like the paper he works for. You can say, if you like, it was natural human curiosity. Every time I've come back to England over the last few months I've seen your name and picture staring out at me over breakfast. Naturally I've wondered how life has treated you——'

'So you dragged me up here to give me a look over!' she interrupted. 'Twelve hours' driving to be inspected like a laboratory specimen!' The T-shirt slipped again but she was heedless. Caught up in her welling anger, she glared at him with blazing eyes and heightened colour. The peace that had been in the room earlier had evaporated, leaving only fury and recriminations.

'That's not what I said!' Brett stared at her for a long moment then he got up abruptly and turned away from her, towards the window. He stared out at the sea and the islands. When he turned to speak, his voice was hard. 'It's a terrible cliché, but you're very beautiful when you're angry. I find it quite disturbing to have you lying in my bed like that. It's not a sight I ever thought to see again.'

The colour flamed higher on her cheekbones. 'Don't evade the issue,' she flung at him.

He took a step back towards her. 'What issue? I've no intention of being lectured on human courtesies by a girl who—as I remember—had very little grasp of such things herself at one time. Neither do I intend to carry on debating why you find yourself here. The fact of the matter is you *are* here, and you might as well accept it with good grace.'

'I don't have to stay here!' Again she flung back the covers and swung her legs down. 'I'll be dressed in five minutes. Then I'd be grateful if you would drive me to my hotel.'

He laughed shortly. 'You must be crazy. You realise you're talking about twenty miles each way over one of the highest passes on the island? And it's no joke driving after dark here, with sheep wandering all over the roads. Why, some of the farmers round here would lynch you for as much as running over an animals' toes! No, you'll stay here tonight.'

He seemed to defeat her at every turn. She hugged herself protectively, looking round.

'Well, I won't stay here—in your bed.'

He walked back and stood dangerously near her.

'I don't remember asking you. At least, not as yet.' He lowered his voice with deliberate provocation. 'But since you've brought the subject up——'

'Don't!' she turned her head, in a futile attempt to block the powerful emanations of his closeness. Then his hand was on her arm, moving slowly up it, under the thin cotton of the wide-sleeved T-shirt.

'Don't what, Janey?' His hand on her shoulder was bringing her round to face him. 'You're still my wife, after all.'

Despite herself she shivered at his touch and her body stirred with desire. Inside her, she knew, there was a deep, deep hunger for Brett—a hunger of years. If she let him near her she would be lost.

'That's all over,' she got out. 'It never started.'

'You might be right,' he observed levelly, 'except in one respect.' He moved his hand to stroke her shoulder and throat. 'And in that particular respect nothing has changed. You know it. And I know it. We both knew it the minute we set eyes on each other again this morning.' His voice had a deep huskiness that sent a shiver across her skin.

'Stop it,' she said tightly. 'Please leave me alone.'

His hand moved to turn her shoulders towards him. 'Do you really mean that?'

'Of course.'

'I don't think you do.'

'How dare you tell me what I mean! What right have you to tell me what I feel or think?'

'No right,' he said, 'only the evidence of my own eyes. And that tells me a different story.'

She forced herself to meet his eyes defiantly, trying to still the trembling that the pressure of his hands aroused. 'I don't know what you mean.'

'I mean this,' he said softly, touching a tremor at the corner of her mouth, 'and this,' his fingers touched a pulse that beat at her neck. 'And this.' One hand lightly feathered the swell of breast, taut against its thin covering.

She shook under his caress and she knew he felt it.

'I'm merely normal,' she got out, squeezing her eyes shut. Only normal. With normal needs and desires. It had been four years since any man had touched her in this way—and that man had been Brett. Inside her was a pent-up lake of need and Brett was threatening to breach its dam. She shifted in his arms to free her breast, but in doing so felt the thud of his heart in his chest. The familiar, forgotten sense of his nearness overwhelmed her with memories.

'Normal enough to enjoy this?' Brett asked tightly, then she felt him draw her closer, and his lips were on hers, firm and cool, unbearably familiar, as they sent piercing shafts of arousal arrowing through her.

For some moments Janey managed to hold herself unmoving in his embrace, but it was a battle lost before it was started. His mouth parted hers and his tongue explored it until she felt herself softening against him, wanting nothing except the moment never to end.

Her mouth gave itself up to his, and her tongue tangled with his as her treacherous arms reached up to enfold the broad muscles of his back.

He shifted to gather her closer, groaning slightly as he kissed her eyes, her nose, the softness below her ears.

'Janey,' he groaned into the hollow of her shoulder. 'You were lovely before; now you're irresistible.'

His lips moved back to kiss her again, fully, deeply, until her body was beating an urgent tattoo of desire for him. Lost, her own hands spread up over his shoulders, into the thickness of his hair.

Hazily her eyes fluttered open. The room was flooded with the last rays of the summer sunset. In the glow his hair was glossy, almost black, but with glinting highlights of copper. She opened her eyes further to drink in its beauty. It was a beauty she knew well—the beauty of Will's hair as he ran and scampered among the apple trees of the garden.

Will! She froze in Brett's arms.

What was she thinking of? Savagely she tore her mouth free. How could she have risked betraying him like this? Just for her own selfish needs! With excessive force she pushed Brett away.

Off guard, he took a step back. His eyes darkened with anger and he pushed a hand through his hair.

'That's a sudden change of heart.' His voice was clipped, expressionless.

'I managed to remember something.'

He took a step back to her and his face was set and hard. 'What, Janey? What were you remembering? How you came chasing down to London after me? How I at least had the decency to marry you? How you ran out after just a couple of weeks?' His voice was rough with suppressed fury.

'Stop it!' She put her hands to her ears, distraught. 'That might be how you see things. It wasn't like that for me. You don't know the half——'

'Oh?' His eyes narrowed dangerously. 'And exactly what is it I don't know?'

'You were glad to see me go,' she flung at him. 'You never contacted me.'

'I didn't know where you were,' he pointed out. 'You didn't have the common decency to let me know. By then I considered you so wilful and unpredictable you could have gone anywhere. And I did send a note to your father's house—to which I got no response.'

She stared at him, silenced, suddenly frightened by this dark gypsy, this familiar stranger with anger in his heart.

She cast her eyes down and to her horror felt tears gathering behind her lids. But she had to be strong! She had to endure! And when she finally drove away from this island, she had to have kept Will's existence a continuing secret, and have Brett out of her life again—for ever.

She blinked rapidly several times and drew a breath.

'I want to go to sleep now. And in the morning I want to go to the hotel as soon as possible. If it's a nuisance for you to drive me then I'll call a taxi. I'm sorry my accident has caused all this trouble.'

He strode to the door, but then he paused, turning.

'It's not the accident that's caused the trouble,' he said harshly. 'It's you, Janey. It always was you.' And he shut the door angrily behind him.

CHAPTER FIVE

'WELL, good morning. I hope you managed to sleep. There's fresh tea in the pot and bread on the side if you want to make yourself toast.'

Brett seemed in high good humour, an astonishing reversal from the night before.

'Yes, thank you.' Janey had managed to sleep, but only as dawn had crept over the murmuring sea outside her window. Most of the night she had lain awake, her body restless with roused longings, and her mind full of uncomfortable thoughts. Then, soon after she had slipped into a doze, the sound of tapping typewriter keys had brought her back to consciousness.

She had dreaded confronting Brett again, and had left coming downstairs as late as she dared, but here he was, whistling cheerfully as he scanned through scattered pages of typescript.

Resentment and amazement fought inside her as she watched him bend over his work. There was something in the fall of his hair that tugged painfully at her heart. Will, bent over his books or toy cars, had exactly the same strong, absorbed profile.

She looked away, out of the window to where piling white clouds were racing across the blue sky.

Brett followed her gaze.

'It's a beautiful morning for a walk, although they

say the weather will change later.'

She looked pointedly down at her tailored trousers and light shoes.

'I'm not here for a rambling holiday.'

'You'll have to do something to pass the time—and Mull isn't exactly thick with art galleries or wine bars.'

'I'd like to go to my hotel.'

'Well, I hope you've booked—this is absolutely the busiest time of the year, and there aren't many hotels on the island.'

'My secretary booked me into the Ferry Hotel. I'm sure they'll extend my booking when they know the circumstances.'

Brett raised a cynical eyebrow, then got up and went out. She heard him dialling, then speaking.

'Nothing at all?' he said. 'Are you sure? Only my visitor's had a car accident. Oh, I see.' There was a pause. 'Well, what about bed and breakfast? Farm accommodation?' Another pause. 'I see. Well, thank you.' He reappeared. She couldn't be sure, but she thought he looked almost smug.

'Nothing,' he said with satisfaction. 'They had two lots of visitors sleeping in their cars on the quay last night.'

'I'll go to Oban.'

'It'll be exactly the same there.'

Janey looked at him angrily.

'Look, it's not my fault. You might as well stay where you know you've got a roof over your head.' She said nothing. He crossed to pour himself another cup of tea. 'You can have my room. I'll move my things. This house can sleep an army. It was built for a family with four children and lots of friends.'

She still sat silent. Her composure felt paper thin, fragile as china. One wrong word and she would crack and break, tears spilling everywhere.

At the *Daily Standard*, confident in her craft, she felt cheerful and strong. But Brett made her feel like the same foolish nineteen year-old who had rushed so heedlessly and disastrously into his bed.

'For goodness' sake, stop looking at me as if I'm some sort of child molester!' he snapped impatiently. 'I promise you that when you shut your door tonight it will stay shut. I can assure you I've got too much pride to go forcing myself on unwilling victims. I've also got no need.'

She turned away, flushing, the implications of his last remark stabbing through her. 'I'd like to get the interview over with this morning. Then I can get away just as soon as my car is ready.'

He sat down at the table, facing her. 'Whenever you're ready.'

She fetched her tape recorder and set it up, glad of the familiar routine. She felt competent again, on firm ground, and she had no intention of giving Brett Britain an easy ride.

She flipped open her notebook. Brett looked surprised. 'My, a tape recorder and notebook—the full works.'

'The tape is merely a back-up—and useful evidence, in case anyone decides to sue,' she said curtly. 'Can we get going?'

He nodded. There was a disconcerting curve to the

corner of his mouth which suggested that he might enjoy any battle that was on the way.

'Tell me what it's like to be a best-selling novelist,' she said bluntly.

'It's very nice,' he parried, with amused understatement. 'I go where I want. Do what I want. It's also hard work. If I haven't done three hours' work before breakfast then the day is ruined.'

'That must put paid to the late nights.'

'I don't need much sleep—as you may remember.'

She looked up from her shorthand and met his look. He was smiling, remembering, she knew, those nights when the birds had begun to sing outside the windows before they had grown sated enough with each other to fall into a perfect sleep. She blushed and pretended to write something in her notebook.

'Where do you live now? Is it still California?'

'For about three months of the year. There's always work to be seen to there. And in London some of the time. And up here, for at least four months each summer.'

'Here?' She was surprised.

'Yes. I own this house. It used to belong to a friend of mine who spent ten years converting it from a ruined shell. Then his wife died, and he couldn't bear the memories.'

'Oh!' She looked up, startled by his matter-of-fact revelation of the tragedy.

'He knew I loved the place as much as he did, so he offered me first refusal. Not that I can make use of it in the way he did. When I go over to the barn and see the canoes lodged up on the beams, or the table-tennis table gathering dust, I feel sad that it's all going to waste. Sometimes I imagine I hear ghostly children's voices about the place.' He looked at her levelly. 'It's the price of being a bachelor, I suppose. In fact, if not on paper.'

Again she felt traitorous colour flooding to her cheeks. Will would love it here, she knew. There would be room to whoop and run about, and scope to learn about birds and flowers. And for a second Brett had sounded almost wistful. She dismissed her uncomfortable train of thought firmly.

'Before we go any further, I ought to check some basic facts,' she said briskly. 'Name?'

'You know that.'

'I mean your full name.'

'Brett Charles McGregor Britain.'

'McGregor?'

'I'm half-Scottish. If you like, I can say I'm returning to my roots by living up here.'

'I wouldn't dream of using such a corny line.'

'Just trying to help.'

'I don't need your help!'

'I can see that.'

Their looks locked in mutual antagonism. Then she ploughed on. 'Age?'

'How old are *you*?'

'Twenty-three.'

'Then I'm thirty-three.'

'Where were you born?'

'In London. I also went to school there, before you ask. Day. Public. Then to Oxford, where I studied politics and economics.'

'Your parents?'

'My father was an engineer. My mother was my mother. We lived a very normal, comfortable life in Wimbledon.'

'And what do they think of their son's success?'

'I don't know. They both died when I was at Oxford.'

'I'm sorry.' Janey hadn't know that, and regretted her crass and abrasive question.

'It doesn't matter. How is your father, by the way?'

She looked up, the question catching her off guard.

'He died three years ago.'

Brett's eyes read hers, saw the shadow of pain in them, and darkened. 'That must have been soon after we——'

'Yes,' she cut in. 'I nursed him that year.'

'You must have had a difficult time. Not the instant success I assumed when I came back to London and saw your name plastered all over the *Daily Standard*.'

'You could say that.' There was deep, unconscious bitterness in her tone. What would he ever know of those lonely months of pregnancy? The solitary joy of Will's birth, or the long struggle to rear the new baby while also nursing her father?

Without the sheltering haven of her family home she would never have survived. Only later had she managed to return to work, and then summon the courage to take the plunge of moving to London. And meanwhile Brett had been who knew where? Sunning himself on the beaches of France or California? She renewed her attack with a vengeance.

'Then you had rather an aimless life, didn't you?

Travelling and taking odd jobs?'

He stopped her question by reaching across the table to grasp her arm. His eyes held hers.

'What do you mean?'

'What——?' She faltered, thrown by his abrupt interruption.

'Why was it so hard, Janey? What happened after we split up? Where did you go and what did you do?'

His look was compelling, full of a dark insistence that demanded an answer. She looked away, frightened he might read the guilty secret in her eyes.

'Why does it matter? It's past history now.'

'I've often wondered—and there was something in your tone——'

She tried to brush the dangerous question aside with a casual shrug. 'I went home, of course. Where would you expect me to go? Then I went back to my old job and after a time I got a break and the chance to join the *Standard*. Now, if we could continue——'

Brett released his fingers slowly, leaving white marks where he had held her arm and his look told her that he knew there was far more to the story than she had said. He leant back with a sigh.

'You were asking about my aimless life,' he said heavily. 'You might call it aimless. I considered it time well spent. I saw a lot of the world, met a lot of people, enjoyed myself—a concept I'm not sure you would understand.'

'What do you mean?'

'I mean you seem so wound up, Janey, so keen to project that tough Fleet Street image, so uptight about everything. I doubt if you can remember what it feels like to let yourself go—I bet it's all work and more work for you these days, and no time to play.'

'Letting myself go never did me any good,' she said bitingly. 'What were you running away from when you took off to the Far East?' His barb had hurt, but she was determined not to show it.

He laughed, not remotely put out by the rudeness of her question.

'Boredom Routine. Oh, and a rather earnest undergraduate called Helen who wanted me to marry her.'

'Did you never consider a proper career? The law, or business?'

'So writing isn't "proper"?' A hint of steel crept into his voice.

'That's what some people might think. Especially some of my readers, who have to do all sorts of unappealing things for a living—hard, dirty jobs, or long hours of shift work.'

He shrugged. 'What am I supposed to do? Beat my breast with woe that I'm a millionaire and take up road digging for a living? I'm profoundly grateful that I've been lucky enough to find a pleasant and profitable way of earning my keep, and I've tried very hard to enjoy the many benefits of it.'

'Tried?' She pounced. 'Does that mean you haven't succeeded?'

'No. I've succeeded—up to a point.'

'What point?'

'You don't let anything go, do you?' There was irritation in his voice now.

'I'm not paid to let things go.'

He said nothing. Janey let the silence grow for a

moment or two. Then she said, 'I want to know if you're happy, Brett.' Her voice was cool, professional, but inside she waited, breathless and trembling, for an answer.

'Why?'

'Because my readers will want to know.' And me, she added silently, I want to know, too. 'They want to know whether the kind of fantasy life they dream of— the travel and parties and women—really bring true happiness, or not.'

'And they hope not,' he said bluntly. 'Because it makes them feel more satisfied with their own humdrum routine.'

She shrugged, 'Maybe.'

'Well, I'm sorry to disappoint them. I enjoy my life very much indeed. I love writing, and I do it very well. I also like living in beautiful and exciting places. I enjoy my friends and I like meeting new people. I enjoy perfect health—shall I go on?'

'And that's happiness?' In front of her eyes came suddenly homelier visions—of Will taking his first tottering steps, or proudly showing his first painting. The perfect, sweet love that she felt when she watched him sleeping like an angel, as she checked his room each night.

'You tell me,' he parried.

'It's more than most people have.'

'And we none of us have everything?' He was watching her closely, she could sense it even though she looked down at her notebook.

'No, we don't——' She felt forced to meet his eyes. He was still scrutinising her, as if he would read her thoughts. She longed to moisten her lips, but she disciplined herself against such betraying signs of emotion.

'What's your happiness, Janey?'

She returned to the safety of her notebook. 'I thought *I* was doing this interview.' He still waited. 'The usual things,' she said at last. 'My job, my friends——'

'Money and success,' he added for her, and she acknowledged the truth of that with a small nod. 'So we're not so very different, are we?' He put his hand across the table and touched her arm lightly. She saw the brown skin of his forearm lightly sprinkled with dark hair. 'Who knows, maybe we're even unhappy in the same ways.' His tone was light, but his touch was searing. She pulled her arm away.

'What about future plans?' she asked him quickly. 'When is your next book coming out? What will it be about?'

He pushed back his chair and went to stand at the window. She glimpsed something like anger on his face. 'In the autumn,' he rattled out. 'It's about here. Mull. In the war. How they mustered the convoys in the lochs. If you want to know more I'll get my publisher to send you a copy.' His voice was hostile.

She replied in kind, stung by his tone. 'You needn't bother. I don't like war stories.'

'Is that it?' he said abruptly. 'Surely you've got enough piffle there to write the regulation five hundred words, or whatever it is. And go easy on the adjectives.'

She stared angrily at his turned back.

'It wasn't *my* idea to do this. It was yours! Or your publisher's! So don't pretend you're above it all. You want the publicity. And no, I haven't finished. There's what we call in the trade 'the romantic interest'. I have to know whether you always live like this——' She cast an arm round the empty kitchen. 'Alone. Or do you have some live-in girlfriend tucked away in California, or London, or wherever it is you call home?'

'Home,' he grated, 'is where I am at any particular given moment. And no, I don't have anyone living with me at the moment. That's not to say I haven't, or won't have in the future. But you can put, if you like, that the idea of the dutiful little wife, for ever sitting at home with supper simmering on the hob, waiting for the typewriter keys to stop tapping, is not my idea of domestic bliss.'

The hard look he gave her underlined the message. It was a stunningly accurate portrait of how she had behaved in their brief weeks together. She felt shot through with anger and humiliation.

'Well, there are plenty of other types to chose from,' she flung back caustically. 'How about a Hollywood starlet? Or one of those female executives that America is supposed to be full of?'

'I suppose you're being deliberately insulting. Or perhaps you just don't know that most starlets have nothing between their ears but pink candyfloss, and most of the female executives I've met are too busy with their self-development to care much about the men in their lives. I like to think I can do a little better than that, thank you——'

She shut her notebook and switched off the tape recorder.

'But you haven't, have you?' The remark was out before she knew it, springing from the deep wells of loneliness and hurt that he had stirred within her.

Colour flushed dully along his cheekbones. 'If I was your editor I'd up-end you and smack your bottom for treating one of your interviewees like that.'

'If I was my editor I wouldn't force me to go and interview my ex-husband. Sorry, my husband.'

They glared at each other in silence for a long moment, until Brett said coldly, 'Any time you want to start proceedings, I won't stand in your way. Now, if you'll excuse me, I've got work to do.'

Her eyes were fixed on him, wide and angry, until, lost for words, she slammed her things together and flounced towards the door, hating the way he sparked the recalcitrant schoolgirl within her.

'I'm sorry,' she said pettishly. 'I thought I had been invited to be a guest in this house. I must have been mistaken.'

'There's no mistake,' he said, and his voice was as cold and smooth as steel. 'You're perfectly welcome to sit in the living-room. You'll find plenty of books to pass the time.' He was sitting down, unclipping his pen. She had no choice but to slam the door and go.

But she could not settle. Through the door came the sound of regular typing. Hadn't she been here before? It was an exact replay of their marriage—Brett working steadily on, while she raged and trembled in another room.

After a time she grabbed her bag and stepped out. The morning air engulfed her in its fresh purity. She paced about the turf. The interview had been a disaster! Oh, she had enough material to write a decent piece, but there had been so many undercurrents she did not understand. That last remark of his had made it plain he would welcome a divorce, but why did he seem so angry and bitter about what must surely be for him a brief and distant chapter of his past history?

She narrowed her eyes and stared across the dancing water. Overhead it was sunny, although dark clouds were banking along the horizon. She knew so very little about him, she realised, not even basic facts like where he had grown up. So how could she hope to untangle the thoughts and feelings of such a complex man?

And what about herself? No matter how many times she vowed to preserve her professional composure, he simply stripped it from her as easily as he might have stripped away her flimsy T-shirt last night, if thoughts of Will had not saved the moment.

Will! She looked at her watch. Somewhere back down the road was a phone box. She could not remember exactly how far it was, but it could only be a couple of miles at most. If she hurried she might just catch him before he left for nursery school.

In fact, swinging along the open road, with the buzzards wheeling overhead and the sea lapping below, she began to feel better than she had at any time since her accident. Slowly her head cleared, until she could think more rationally about Brett, and all that had passed between them since her arrival.

It was shameful but true, she realised, that she had never paused to consider what their marriage had meant to him. She had assumed at the time that he was glad to see her go, and then Will's birth and her father's death had driven almost everything except selfish survival from her mind.

She had never dreamt that he could have been hurt by her departure, but the bitter edge to some of his remarks showed otherwise. Although, she reflected cynically, it would have been his pride that would have taken the battering. Brett was without doubt an intensely proud man and having, as he put it, had the decency to marry her, he would have hated to have his generosity thrown back in his face.

Not that she had ever really understood why he had done it. He was a fundamentally decent man, she had always known that, but she had never asked for, or expected, a gold band on her finger, and had been overwhelmed with delighted surprise to find it there. Her steps faltered.

Brett had behaved very decently towards her, there was no doubt about it . . . Could the same be said of her own decision to conceal Will's existence from him?

She was alarmed at the turn her thoughts had taken. After all, it wasn't a question of what was right and proper! What counted was survival. If she was to survive as Will's competent, caring mother, then there could be no room in their lives for someone who turned her into an unstable teenager again. And certainly no room for anyone who just might choose to try to claim Will from her!

The telephone box was much further along the lonely road than she remembered, but the long hike was worth it for the sound of Will's cheerful voice. She was far more concerned than him, she realised, at her prolonged absence, and his casual 'Bye' made her realise for the first time that he was inevitably beginning to grow out of that deep closeness that had marked their first insulated years. It was a natural thing, but the new realisation tinged her sadness.

Yet turning back she faced a new worry altogether. The sky ahead of her was massed with inky clouds, and the wind, which had been a pleasant breeze on her back, was now blowing relentlessly on her face. It was a struggle to walk against it, and when the rain finally came there was no shelter to be found anywhere.

Within minutes she was wet, then soaked, then completely drenched. There was nothing to be done except plough on, weary and surprisingly chilled.

The sound of wet tyres on the road made her look up, blinking against the streaming water.

'Get in.' It was Brett.

'I know, I know,' she said, shutting the door. 'I'm a fool.'

'You're the one who said it.' He still sounded clipped and angry.

He cut the engine and turned in his seat to look at her. Water streamed down her face, making her blink and sniff, and ran from her hair in cold trickles down her neck.

'Oh, Janey——!' The anger was gone from his

voice now, replaced by an amused exasperation as he took in her bedraggled appearance. Smile lines creased the corners of his eyes, softening his face and warming his gaze.

Something tight rose in her throat. She suddenly longed to hurl herself against him and be warmed and comforted by his embrace. Hurriedly she sniffed hard and began to search in her bag for a tissue.

'You *are* in a state,' he said bluntly, 'here.' He reached for a cloth from the back of the car and gently wiped the worst of the rain from her face before handing it to her to mop her neck and hair. 'I've got an old sweater here. It's quite long enough to make a passably decent dress. Do you want to put it on?'

She shook her head vehemently.

'Well, at least put this round you.' He tucked a travelling rug round her shoulders with hands that were deft but gentle. She had forgotten this side of him, she realised with surprise, burying it beneath memories of passion and anger, yet when they had been together she had come to treasure his kindness and warmth, had dreamed of the loving father he would become to their future children——She shut her eyes tightly, blocking her thoughts.

'It's a good job you didn't decide to stroll off up a mountain. I'd never had found you then—and people have been known to die of exposure on these hills, even in summer.'

'I didn't think. I never dreamt the weather could change so fast. It was foolish to go off like that without even a coat.'

'Then why do it?'

'It's always easier to be wise after the event.'

'You mean like running after me to London, I suppose? Or getting married? Marry in haste, repent at leisure?'

His tone was light, but something in it made her pause in mopping her hair and seek his eyes.

'I don't know,' she said hesitantly. 'If you like.'

'Do you regret what happened?' he persisted. She paused. The rain was drumming a fierce tattoo on the outside of the car, and inside the windows were steamed up with their breath. It was an enclosed, private world, with nowhere to run and hide.

Did she regret it? In her mind's eye she saw Will's eager, loving face. Nothing would ever make her regret his precious existence. Nor those days and nights of intense happiness that had preceded it—before the bliss had turned sour.

'I don't know,' she repeated slowly. 'It did happen, so there's no point even thinking about it. Why does it matter now, anyway?'

The smile lines faded from his eyes and his look hardened.

'Perhaps you're right,' he said shortly, reaching for the engine key.

'What about you?' she suddenly found herself blurting out. 'Do you regret it?'

His eyes went over her. 'We shouldn't have married,' he said slowly, and her heart fell like a stone. His tone was that of a man who had long ago decided his position on the subject. 'It was the wrong thing, at the wrong time.'

'I see.'

'Do you, Janey? I wonder.'

'I see enough.' A shudder suddenly racked her. He looked at her with fresh concern, her dripping hair and the clothes plastered to her skin, transparent with rain.

'And this is certainly the wrong time for this sort of conversation,' he said briskly, starting the car. 'You'd better have a hot bath when you get in.'

'I'll be all right,' she said, shivering.

'It's an order. You'll have one even if I have to strip you off myself and dump you in the tub.' He smiled grimly. 'Come to that, I might actually enjoy doing that——'

He wasn't joking.

'I'll have a bath,' she agreed hastily.

Later, warmed by the steaming water and wrapped in an old plaid dressing-gown Brett had found for her, Janey sat on the wide window-ledge of the sitting-room, feet tucked up, watching the wind and rain lash the landscape.

'I really was stupid,' she murmured to herself, seeing the cloud trail in almost at sea level.

Brett, sitting across the room, put down his book.

'You were—after all, there's a telephone in the hall.'

They were both speaking quietly. Brett got up and stood in front of the fire that burned in the open grate, his hands thrust into his jean pockets. She watched his broad figure, the even profile, the contained and thoughtful eyes. It was silent in the room, and frighteningly intimate. She was suddenly scared of what could be said, of secrets that clamoured to be let out.

Her gaze flickered desperately round the room, the books, the prints, the faded cushions on the homely scttcc. 'You can see why they built the walls so thick,' she said hastily. 'It's blowing a gale out there, but in here you barely even hear it.'

He looked at her as if she had not spoken. There was a look she could not read in his eyes.

'Those friends again, I suppose?'

'If it was, what does it matter to you?'

'Just intrigued—matters of mystery always catch my imagination, and you seem bent on being as mysterious as possible.'

'There's no mystery—I went out for a walk, and while I was walking I decided to do something useful and aim for a phone box where I could make a call. It's perfectly natural to want a definite goal. I might just as easily have decided to try and reach the top of the little mountain across the road, but, as you pointed out earlier it's a good job I didn't.'

Despite her best efforts to keep her voice neutral there was an air of defensiveness in her tone.

Brett moved across the room and poured himself a whisky, lifting the bottle towards her in silent question. She shook her head. He sat down again. Beneath the dressing-gown her toes were curled tight, responding to the tension that hummed in the room.

After a silence that seemed eternal he said, 'I told you a lot about my life this morning. Perhaps you should return the compliment. Why don't you tell me something about yourself, Janey? What do you like to do when you're not working?'

'There's nothing to tell. Sometimes I go to concerts, or films. But mainly I live very quietly.'

'That doesn't sound like the girl I remember. I would have said you were looking for anything but the quiet life. What's happened to change it?'

'Nothing—perhaps you never knew me very well.'

'Perhaps not. But chasing after me to London like you did—surely that's the impulse of a risk-taker, someone who would rather gamble all they have on the tide of the moment than let life flow past their locked door?'

'My work supplies all the risks I need. And, anyway, I've never done anything like that either before or since.'

'I'm very flattered to hear it. Why exactly did you do it, anyway, Janey? I've never found a satisfactory answer.'

She felt like quarry being stalked by an expert hunter. One way or another he managed to back her into corners where there was nowhere to hide.

'Perhaps I was a fool,' she said shortly, wanting only to push him away, back on to safer ground. 'Why do you do anything when you're nineteen?'

His mouth tightened and he threw back the last of his whisky in one go.

'Well, isn't that just what you said?' she continued. 'The wrong thing, at the wrong time? If you want to know the truth, I've never been able to work out why I did it, what I was thinking about. All I know for sure is that it all proved a great mistake.'

'So you do regret it.' His words echoed their earlier

exchange in the car, as the rain hammered down. 'You hoped never to see me again.'

She met his eyes, her chin lifting. 'No one in the world could call our marriage a success. I don't know why we even need to discuss it. It happened and now it's over. There's been—what's the phrase?—a lot of water under the bridge since then.'

Janey forced her voice to sound clipped and cold, although the way their glances tangled made her quake and tremble inside.

He held her look steadily until the tension in the room seemed to rise as high as the wind which howled mutedly about the house. The only sound in the room was the crackle and splutter of the logs in the hearth. Eventually Brett got up and crossed to the fire.

'My God, but you've grown tough,' he said.

She said nothing, but she could not look away from him. If only he knew how she really felt—yet tough was what she had to be, for the sake of Will. But Brett's dark regard was powerful and intense, and a current flowed between them that no words could deny.

'Come here,' he said suddenly.

Her lips parted in surprise. She wanted to protest, but could not find her voice. Something deep inside her trembled.

'I said, come "here".'

As if sleepwalking, her feet found the floor and she went to him. He made no move to touch her, but his eyes on her face felt like an assault on her senses.

'Janey, you're my wife, and I still want you,' he said bluntly. His eyes, going over her, left her in no doubt of his meaning. She said nothing. She could not speak, her throat was as dry as a desert.

'You feel the same. I don't know why, but I'm certain of it.'

Still she could find no words, nor could her eyes leave his face.

He said, 'I can hardly bear to be in the same room as you like this. We both sit here resolutely looking away, or crossing verbal swords, trying to pretend we're not striking sparks off each other, and all the time the tension is building up for a major storm.'

She looked down, but he put a hand under her chin, forcing her head up again.

'You seem to want to pretend nothing's ever happened between us. That we've never managed to give each other pleasure as well as pain——'

His look flooded her cheeks with colour, as it roused vivid memories of the sheer intensity of that pleasure.

'Why are you doing this?' she cried out. 'I'm not trying to deny anything. But why drag up everything that's passed?' She tried to block the memories with words.

'Why? Isn't it obvious? You and I are stuck here together for some days. We can't go on like this. It's like a pressure cooker.'

'So what do you suggest?'

His hand moved from her chin to hold her shoulder: 'Our marriage might not have been worth the paper it's written on, but it had its moments. We managed to please each other in bed, if nowhere else. And that's more than many couples do.'

His gaze was too compelling. She stared past him, at

the flickering flames, adrift on a wild sea of clashing emotions.

'Janey.' It was a command to meet his eyes. Her blue gaze flickered purple. 'Why fight it?'

'Nothing's the same——' she cried.

'No. You're older, more beautiful than ever. You almost frighten me with that cool poise you've acquired. There aren't many women on Mull who drive fast cars and wear expensive designer clothes.'

His eyes invited her to smile with him, but she fought against it. 'There must be plenty in California, or France, or wherever.'

'Maybe, but not like you. You've always been different. I knew it from the moment you walked wide-eyed into my hotel room. There's always been that chemistry between us that won't go away, no matter how hard we try.'

'I hadn't noticed you trying very hard.'

A small quirk crooked his mouth.

'Why should I? It seems to me the world wouldn't come to an end if we shared bed as well as board for a day or so. Even the Highland puritans of Mull could hardly object to a man making love to his own wife.'

'But it wouldn't be love, would it?' she said bitterly. 'It would be——' she paused, '—sex. Just sex. Just like it always was. I was young enough to muddle up the two in the past, but I won't make the same mistake twice.'

An angry line marked his forehead at her words, and his fingers tightened on her shoulder. He paused, then he said, 'Sex isn't a sin. You're talking like one of those puritans. It can be, just like anything else, if it's done with malice, or cruelty, or deceit. But it can also be a blessing, a comfort, warmth on a cold day——'

'Like a hot toddy, you mean. No, thank you! It isn't like that for me, and it never will be! If I want warmth, I'll put on an extra sweater. Sex means more than that to me. It's too personal, too dangerous——' She faltered, her thoughts flying to Will.

His eyes glinted. 'I don't remember such high-mindedness before. That day you arrived at my London flat, remember? Maybe my memory's faulty, but I can't recall any qualms on your part, any moral angst——'

'Stop it! It's all in the past! It's over. Finished.'

'It might be, but that doesn't mean it never happened. You can't just run away from painful memories, Janey, or the consequences of your own actions, however much you might want to.'

She laughed bitterly. 'You've no idea how funny that is.' His eyes bored into her, intent. She scrabbled to regain her composure. 'I just don't see the point of resurrecting old ghosts,' she said feebly.

'They're not old, they're all around us. Can't you feel them?' He pushed back his hair. 'God, I'll remember till the day I die the moment I opened my front door and saw you standing there. So young and vulnerable. Impossibly beautiful. I knew I should shut the door, leave you standing there, untouched, undamaged. But you stepped forward with such a look in your eyes, such apprehension and impulsiveness swimming in those blue eyes, that I knew I was lost.'

She was held by his eyes, mesmerised, her heart

hammering to know he had felt that way. But his voice continued relentlessly. 'Do you remember what happened then, Janey?' She shuddered at the rasp in his tone. 'I took your hand and led you inside. I don't remember you holding back. I don't remember you saying "Oh no, sorry, Brett. I only stopped by because I was passing". No. You let yourself be led. You stood close in front of me, face turned up, just like you're standing now. And when I made no move to hold you, you put your hands up to my shoulders. Then I took you in my arms and kissed you——' She longed to shout for him to stop, but she was powerless, pulled back with him into that vortex of powerful memories that she had shut out for so long. '——and I forgot you were nineteen, a girl from the country, a virgin. You were the kind of woman a man dreams of, so passionate and yielding that nothing on earth could have stopped me making love to you. You do remember, do you, Janey, what happened when our lips touched? It was madness, a raging fire. I've never forgotten taking you to bed, the sweetness of your body and the trusting openness of your longing.'

She flushed and lowered her eyes. His words were heated, but his voice seemed cold.

'I wanted to make it good for you, but I needed you too much, too soon. I made you cry out—sometimes I've heard that cry in my dreams, and felt myself a monster.'

'I was a fool,' she whispered. 'You should have sent me away.'

'You made it impossible,' he said. 'That day and all the days after. I'll tell you the truth, Janey—there have been women before you and since, but there's never been anything like those days we spent together. God knows why, but no woman has inflamed me the way you did, and no woman has sated me so completely.'

His words stirred her, more deeply and dangerously than anything else since they had met again. She flung out an angry response to shield herself from them. 'And that's why you dragged me up here? In the hope of a brief Highland fling for the sake of old times? What did you think, Brett? That one smouldering glance from you and I'd melt right back to the foolish, love-blinded teenager I once was?'

'Why, you little——' He bit off his words as if frightened of what he might say. Then he gripped her firmly by the arms. 'As it happens, that wasn't the reason. But it could be like that, it could very well be.'

His fingers tightened and she knew in a split second she had goaded him too far.

'That teenager isn't as nearly deeply buried as you'd like her to be,' he said scathingly. 'And from the vibrations you're giving out, it would barely take a glance, smouldering or otherwise, to resurrect her.'

She flung back her head with a flimsy attempt at defiance, but the gesture simply raised her lips to his. Before she realised what he was doing he was kissing her ruthlessly, opening her mouth to his without mercy until the thrusting demands of his tongue made her moan against him.

His arms were bands around her, holding her captive. His body moulded itself to hers with hard and urgent desire. One imperious hand left her shoulders and moulded the curve of her spine and swell of her buttocks, pulling her against him.

She longed to resist. There was no caring in his embrace, only the will to dominate. But her wanting arms were tightening about him. Her lips were open to his, and her body drummed with an upsurge of desire as urgent as his own imperative need.

She did not protest when he parted her robe and found the curves of her breasts, and when his fingers explored their hard tips, she cried out against his mouth.

Roughly he pushed her back against the cushions of the sofa, his whole being concentrated in a harsh determination to claim her for himself again. He pushed aside the dressing-gown, leaving her naked to his gaze. Then his lips were on her breasts, caressing until she moaned beneath him and began to reach for him heatedly, tugging his shirt free so she could touch his naked flesh.

At that moment he stood up and stepped back.

'No you don't.'

It took a moment for the shock to break through. Then she sat up abruptly, pulling the dressing-gown about her. Her lips were red, her hair fell in disarray, and her body still throbbed its needs.

'Why——' She felt flooded with shame and humiliation and remorse. 'You can't just——'

'Can't I?'

She looked at him mutely.

'I think I've proved my point. Our ghosts are neither dead or buried. I won't cause you further inconvenience by pressing home my advantage.' His lips twisted sardonically, in the certain knowledge that that was just what she had desired.

'What am I meant to say?' she said shakily. 'Congratulations?'

'No, just admit that you want me every bit as much as I still want you.'

Angry humiliation flooded through her. She stood up, tossing back her hair.

'Yes, all right, I do! When you force me to be aware of it! But it's in one way, and one way only! You're a very attractive man, Brett, and a skilful enough lover! No doubt if you want to come breaking down my bedroom door and overwhelming me with your charms, then you'll succeed. But all there is between us—all there's ever been—is a physical attraction. I want you. I admit it. Just as I always wanted you. But as a man, as a stud, not as a person! That's how it was in the past, and that's how it always will be!'

Tears threatened to fog her view of him as he stood before her, a granite-like figure with a gaze as hard and cold as the rain pounding at the window.

'Oh!' She choked back tears and ran from the room, only just gaining the privacy of her bedroom before the racking sobs shook her.

CHAPTER SIX

'I NEED to go to Dervaig to get supplies,' Brett said. 'You can either come or stay.'

It was the next morning, another wild, wet, stormy day. From the moment Janey had come downstairs it was clear he had withdrawn from her utterly. When she glanced at him she saw a dark, strong face that was closed like a mask, and eyes that gave nothing away.

He was pulling on boots and a heavy green oiled jacket. She looked out, but there was nothing to see except tearing rain and shimmering clouds.

All night she had lain sleepless, tormented by her thoughts. At one moment, in the dark hours, the need to have his arms about her again had grown so strong that she feared she would run down the passage to his rooms. Only by fixing her mind firmly on Will had she been able to keep from such madness.

But mad was what she felt she would go, if she was left alone with her thoughts any longer.

'I'll come.'

Wordlessly he handed her a spare jacket and set off through the bucketing rain without even looking round to see if she was following.

In the car he said curtly, 'There won't be much to see—except some of the island's finest scenery. And

I'm not sure how much that would interest a city girl like yourself.'

'I only live in London because my work's there!' The implied contempt in his remark stung her. 'If I were a millionaire author, I'd probably choose to spend my time in somewhere just like this.'

'Millionaire author! I see you already see me through the eyes of your readers. You could spend today more profitably hacking out the required few hundred words of clichés to package me for public consumption.'

'I did that yesterday afternoon. I'll phone it in today. They need it so they can start serialising your latest book—and pushing up your inflated bank balance—next Monday. Anyway——' she pressed on regardless in her anger, '—it's still a mystery why you decided to break your public silence. If you so much hate being packaged like this, why the sudden change of heart?'

'It's very simple. My publishers are nice people. Occasionally I try to make them happy by falling in with their plans. And I still had some faith in your integrity, despite your meteoric rise to stardom— what helped you on your way, incidentally? The casting couch?'

'That's a disgusting thing to say!'

'Maybe. All I know is that you fell into bed pretty rapidly with at least one of your subjects—and one you didn't much like, according to your own account. In the light of that little revelation almost anything is possible.'

She flushed furiously. 'If you must know, I was just

lucky. After I went back to my old job, Frank Evans, the Deputy Editor, left to join the *Standard*, and when they needed a new features writer he put in a word for me.'

'So—rags to riches overnight. Cinderella went to the ball.'

'It wasn't a ball, it was—is—damn hard work.'

'You mean you don't haunt the inns and taverns of Fleet Street? No glittering first nights? No socialite parties?'

'I have to get home at nights,' she snapped, then bit off her words. But it was too late. For the first time since they had begun the drive, Brett turned to look at her. His eyes scoured her face.

'I see.'

'No, you don't.'

'Then perhaps you ought to put me straight.'

'I don't have to explain my private life to you or anyone else.'

'I could remind you that you are my wife.'

'In name only! You can have a divorce for the asking—in fact, I don't understand why you haven't!' Pain shafted through her as she spoke. She looked abruptly away, but she could feel the bitterness between them as clearly as she could feel the car's heater warming her legs.

'I've never felt the need,' he said, after a moment. 'It may surprise you to know that it wouldn't be a decision I would take lightly. And I've never had the slightest desire to marry again.' He flashed her a dark look. 'What about you?'

'Me neither,' she muttered, glancing at him, then away.

His remark had surprised her. She had always assumed their brief and hasty union could, probably would, be ended by him without a second thought. She longed to probe his thoughts further, but his dark mood stopped her, as did thoughts of Will. The more they talked, challenged and argued, the less hope she would have of keeping their son's existence hidden. So the questions that formed in her head remained unvoiced, and she turned her head to look out of the window.

Outside, the landscape was spectacular. Under stormy skies, small islands studded the dark and churning sea. The few houses along the road were sheltered by trees, bent and gnarled from the sea gales, and as they turned inland and began to climb, rain-soaked moors of heather and peat opened up all around. The rolling clouds were reflected in inky pools, whose surfaces were blown like silk rippled by the wind.

She drank in the powerful scene like a thirsty man. The wide sky and menacing mountains were bigger, older than her small worries and emotions.

In London she hurtled from job to home with barely time to glance up at the sky. There was never time to think clearly, or to relish Will's steady growing. She sighed, deeply and unconsciously, as the full weight of her relentless responsibilities came down on her. Brett looked across at her, but for a brief moment she was unaware of him.

Maybe her friend Ann was right, she thought.

Maybe she should find a man, a nice, decent man, who would be a husband for her and a father for Will. Ann often invited her upstairs to relaxed, informal supper parties where one or other eligible bachelor was served up to try and tempt her.

But she didn't want a nice man. The man she wanted was strong and cynical, and filled with contempt for her, and if he still wanted her at all then it was in one way, and one way only.

The car began to swing down to a small village cupped in a bowl of hills. Brett said, 'I'll drop you at the pub while I sort out a few things. I'm sure in your job you're quite used to waiting in bars alone.'

'That's fine,' she said curtly, 'Is there a phone?'

'Checking with those friends of yours again?'

'I thought I might as well use the time to phone my copy over,' she lied.

'You could have done that at home, without the inconvenience of a pay phone.'

'It's no problem. I've got a telephone credit card.'

'I see. Equipped for every eventuality. You really are quite armour-plated these days, Janey, I wonder if anyone ever gets near you?' Brett stopped the car.

She got out and stared back at him with hostility. 'You don't have a clue about me!' she cried out. 'I doubt if you ever did?' And she slammed the door hard before he could even turn in her direction.

The phone was engaged. She nursed a glass of lager in the almost empty bar and watched a young girl, the owner's daughter, struggle with touching ineptitude to try and pacify her obviously new baby. Will had been a good-tempered infant, but she could still remember the blind panic she had felt when he'd struggled and cried for no apparent reason.

Now she ached to hear his voice telling her his latest news. At the fourth attempt she got through. It was cold in the stone hallway, and the wind was howling and battering at the door so that she could hardly hear.

'Will, darling, it's Mummy.'

'Hello.'

'Are you all right? Are Ann and John looking after you nicely?'

'Yes.'

She could picture him marshalling his thoughts, carefully preparing to release a nugget of information. 'We went to the museum yesterday. There was a space rocket.'

'A space rocket! That must have been exciting. Was it the Science Museum?'

'Yes. Thomas, from school, wanted to touch it. But the man said you couldn't.'

'Well, you mustn't touch things in museums unless someone says you can.'

'There were trains, too, and a room with crayons, for drawing.' There was another pause. 'We had crumpets for tea. With jam. But I just had butter.'

'Mmm. Lovely.' There was another pause. She sensed the disembodied conversation was a strain for him. 'Will, love, I'll be home as soon as I can. Will you give everyone my love?'

'OK.'

'Bye, bye, my darling. I'm missing you dreadfully.'

'Bye.'

'Bye.' She put the phone down slowly, loathe to give up the link with her dark-eyed, beautiful son.

She turned away slowly, her eyes full of sadness. Brett was standing in the doorway. She had no idea how long he had been there, but she knew that from where he was standing he would have clearly heard every word she'd uttered! She gasped with dismay.

His look told her that her last words, at least, had not escaped him, but instead of the cutting words she braced herself for, he simply turned and went on into the bar.

She had no choice but to follow him, her heart hammering furiously at the thought her secret might be out. But all he said, scathingly, was, 'As I thought—some friend!' before turning away to order.

But before the barman could pull his pint, a telephone behind the bar suddenly shrilled. The man turned away to answer it. His face changed as he listened, then he spoke a few abrupt words and put it down.

To Brett he said, 'The team's been called out. Some daft beggars have gone and got themselves lost up on the top there.' He nodded towards the door. 'They should have come off the hills by now, but there's no sign of them. They've got a bit of camping equipment, but no storm gear. I was going to say lucky you were over here, but you won't have your stuff with you——'

'I have. It's always in the car.' Janey looked from one to the other. Brett's face told her that she was quite forgotten. 'Do you want me to go and get anyone else?' The men talked rapidly about necessary arrangements. Already the door was swinging open to admit others. She retreated to a distant corner seat and sat silently watching. They were all big, burly men, calm and confident, the sort that any lost wanderer would be glad to see striding towards him.

Especially Brett, whose broad shoulders looked strong enough for anything. She thought achingly of all the times she had worried alone about Will, when he had been ill or upset. How wonderful it would have been to lean into those arms and be comforted! Briefly she closed her eyes and remembered the rock-like strength of his embrace, but the sound of jangling keys brought her back to the present.

'Here,' said Brett, 'you'd better take the car back. God knows how long all this will take. Can you manage? It's a powerful motor.'

'Of course.' She looked at his stern face and jarringly returned to reality. Brett had no warmth to offer her, only a powerful sexual chemistry that led to nothing except heartbreak and loss. 'Follow the road we came in by, and take it slowly on those bends at the top of the pass.'

He followed her out and heaved a rope, some boots and a battered green rucksack from the car. She sat at the wheel and methodically checked the unfamiliar controls, Brett leaned down to the open window. They were close again, their eyes meeting with that same unfathomable complexity.

'OK?'

Janey nodded. 'How will you get back?'

'One of the lads will run me over when we get back. God knows when that will be.'

Involuntarily she looked up to where heavy black clouds swept down, obscuring the mountain peaks. 'It looks awful up there.'

'It probably is. This rain will be ice and hail on the tops.'

'Will it be dangerous?'

He shrugged. 'Conditions can get treacherous. It depends where those lunatics have got themselves to.' He straightened up and the wind blew his hair about. Then he bent again. 'I heard this morning that your car might be almost ready. If by any chance I'm not back before you need to catch the ferry, take the car and leave the keys at the hotel.'

'You could be that long?'

'Anything can happen.' She looked up at him from her driver's seat, her eyes huge and haunted with strain, her cheeks pale and her bottom lip caught up with worry.

'You will take care?'

His face set as if to give her a bitter answer, but instead his eyes softened and he bent abruptly and kissed her, a short, harsh, tearing kiss that shot her through with anguish.

'Goodbye, Janey,' he said, 'Look after my car.'

Goodbye, she thought miserably, as she drove carefully back over the wild moors. Goodbye, maybe for ever. The curtain of low cloud dragging across the sky exactly matched her ragged thoughts, the lowering landscape mirrored precisely how she felt inside.

There was a space inside her ribs that ached with pain and emptiness. She felt battered by wild and conflicting emotions. Goodbye. The word seemed to echo hollowly in her head, over and over again.

She had dreaded meeting Brett again. But always, deep inside—so deep that Janey only now acknowledged it to herself—she had always known it would happen sometime.

Oh, she had pretended otherwise, as she had carefully built her life so there was no room in it for him or any man, but subconsciously she had been sure that at some point the forceful magnet of their mutual attraction would bring them on to a collision course again.

Now it had happened, but although the attraction was as powerful as ever, the antagonism was greater. Their glances only had to lock and they were striking angry blows at each other. It made her feel drained and hopeless, while he seemed to feel only dislike for the hard and calculating woman he so clearly thought her to be. She longed to be able to open up to him, to argue and explain herself more clearly, but Will stopped her words as effectively as if he were here, with his little hand clamped firmly over her lips. And even if she did, she thought miserably, what then? There was no future in a relationship based solely on sexual passion, and beyond that, and a general kind of curiosity about her life, Brett obviously cared nothing for her at all.

Back in the safety of the kitchen, away from the

wildness of the weather, she unpacked the supplies Brett had bought and made a mug of coffee. Then she sat staring at the tossing waves, trying to unravel her thoughts.

It was hard, and it hurt. It had been years, she realised now, since she had honestly faced the feelings buried inside herself, perhaps not since the day she had impetuously slammed the door on their brief marriage.

Brett had sent her a note after their first meeting. She could still remember it by heart.

'My sweet Janey,' it ran. 'If only you were older, more sure of who you are, or I younger, or we weren't a hundred miles apart, there might be a future for us. But just now there isn't. Who knows. Maybe later? Till then, I shall always think of you, Brett.'

She had carried it round all day, looking at it endlessly, until the creases in the thick, white paper were worn right through. The firm writing made her irrationally furious. As if nineteen were that young! she thought angrily. Or twenty-nine so old! And how dared he pass up something so obviously unique and precious with just a few casual words?

What had happened after that was still lost in a headlong daze. Somehow she had found herself packing a case, taking a train, finding a way to his Kensington flat. She could remember trembling on his doorstep, appalled at what she had done. And she could remember his look—puzzled, angry, delighted—as he took in her presence.

This time he had not been able to resist her. Their

first night together had been one of the most exquisite times of their life. Then there had been a blissful, unreal week where they had barely left the flat, and he had worked and eaten the meals she had cooked for him, and they had talked and made love endlessly, all night and sometimes all day.

At the end of that week he had asked her, abruptly, 'What about your father?'

She had shrugged, made light of the question. 'He knows where I am. He would be marginally less worried, I suppose, if it was all above board and legal.'

'Right then, we'll get married.'

And they had, at the local register office, and afterwards that night, lying beside him in the dark, listening to his deep, even breathing, she had thought she could never be happier.

Her eyes scanned the wild Scottish sea without seeing. Oh, she had been young! So very, very young!

Quite when things had started to go wrong she could not say. But slowly, over the next few weeks, she had grown bored with shopping and cooking and tidying Brett's bachelor flat. She roamed the London streets during the long hours when Brett applied himself to his typewriter, feeling increasingly lonely and isolated among the crowds that pushed uncaringly past her on the pavements.

She began to miss her friends, her home, her job, and wondered if her resignation, impulsively typed and sent on her first morning in London, had been too hasty.

Only when she was lying with Brett, naked in his arms, or talking with him through to the early hours of the morning, did she feel whole and happy again, but his life was hectic and crowded. He was involved in films, and in television versions of his books. He had people to see, places to go. Somehow she never seemed to become part of his wider life, yet she no longer had any life of her own.

She was bored, anxious and increasingly miserable. Domestic bliss tipped gradually into domestic irritation, and minor squabbles grew into full-scale rows.

Brett suggested she should find a job, but her first few attempts failed, and she lacked the courage to go on. She felt her lack of experience and unfinished training too keenly to impress cynical editors who curtly answered her tentative phone calls.

Sometimes their entire marriage seemed to her like a speeded-up film of marital breakdown. Most people took a decade or so to court and marry and then grow apart, but the whole history of their relationship spanned only six weeks.

The final row, when it came, was no different from all the others. Brett had wanted to work. She had wanted his company, preferably outside the flat which had grown to seem like an elegant prison. Bitter words were shouted as they stared at each other in mutual hostility, both appalled by the situation they had locked themselves into. And suddenly she had turned, picked up her bag and walked out. Just like that.

It was her last vision of Brett. Barefoot, in jeans

and a white T-shirt, standing in the door to his study, a thunderous look on his face as he surveyed the furious, shouting redhead who was his child bride.

She had been stupid, utterly and completely foolish! Yet Brett had hardly been blameless, she thought. So wrapped up had he been in his writing that he had not seen, or not wanted to see, just how vulnerable and alone she felt in that new life.

Back at her father's house she had longed for some word or gesture that would pull her back to him, but only the briefest of polite notes, 'hoping she was all right, and would manage to piece her life together again', accompanied the returned case of clothes that arrived a week later.

Those first few weeks had been wretched, so much so that it had taken her a long time to realise that her misery had a physical dimension, most particularly in the mornings when dizziness and nausea greeted her first steps out of bed.

Almost simultaneously her father's health had declined sharply. His needs, and later those of her new son, had taken all her energies. In those years she had suffered and sacrificed and grown, and there had never been time to do anything but bury her brief marriage beneath the more pressing needs of the present.

But meeting Brett again had broken down all those barriers she had erected against her own feelings. Now she had to acknowledge how much she still yearned for him, longed to throw herself in his arms and have him make passionate love to her.

Yet it was more than that, so much more. She

wanted to lean on his strength, and be comforted by him. And she wanted to comfort him, too. In those glimpses he had allowed her on his private thoughts she had sensed a quest that remained unfinished, a bitterness that she longed to ease with warmth and care.

No, not care. She put down her mug and stared sightlessly at the loch. Not care, love. She had loved Brett from their first meeting, had always done, and did so still. She loved him so completely, so utterly, that no other man could mean anything to her.

Brett, she thought despairingly, Brett out on the rain-lashed mountainside. She imagined him struggling doggedly out through the worst of conditions, his mind set only on the rescue. When he did something, he did it with all of himself, every last ounce of energy. When he wrote, all that existed for him were the words in front of him. When he made love—no! Stop, she told herself, forcing her thoughts to turn away from that painful track.

Brett was her man, as she had known he was from that first meeting. But what lay between them now was too tangled to be straightened, too damaged to be mended.

Janey stood up and went to the window, her eyes watching a fishing boat labouring slowly towards a safe anchorage, but her thoughts were far away. Far away with Will, their son. She loved Brett, yet she was deliberately concealing their son from him, just as, despite her deep love for Will, she was keeping his father from him. She had kidded herself it was a necessity, but in the new clarity that lit her thoughts it seemed more like a criminal offence.

She chewed her lip till it hurt, but found no way out of the maze she had got herself into. She and Brett could not co-exist with any sort of equanimity, so how could they possibly share a child? That demanded harmony, agreement, generosity—none of which were present in their hostile relationship. And, anyway, how could she ever find the courage to break the news to him? His fury at her deception would know no bounds, she was certain.

The wind, battering with renewed force at the window, brought her back to the present. She felt utterly hopeless. She loved Brett. She should tell him about Will. That was as far as all her thinking had got her. But she did not know how she could make Brett return her love, or how she would ever find the courage to confess to Will's existence, or how she could cope with her life after that.

For the sake of something to do, she phoned the garage and heard the news Brett had intimated earlier. They had been lucky with the spare parts, and had managed to get hold of them in Oban, after all. Her car would be ready by midday tomorrow. Her spirits lifted a little. She had no solution to her problems, but at least now she could run away from them.

Then she phoned the office and began to dictate her interview with Brett.

'Brett Britain, comma, the world's most exclusive best-selling author, comma, is the epitome of the private man, full stop,' she intoned slowly. 'This week he gave me the first interview he has granted since his spectacular rise up the best-seller lists, but although the words flowed smoothly from his lips they concealed rather than revealed the man behind the novelist——'

Laboriously she read out the rest of the piece, knowing from experience the exact pace needed to match the copy-taker's pounding typewriter. When she had finished she asked to be put through to the Features Department, and told them the piece was on its way to them.

'Is it any good?' asked Reg Dale, the Features Editor, bluntly.

'It's fair. He's too clever to give anything away. Although I did pick up one or two bits. He seems to have a bit of hankering for a family, although I don't think it's very serious. There's a good line or two about the lonely millionaire in the house built for children—the unused boats, and the dust on the table-tennis table, that sort of thing——' Her voice tailed off, stopped by a lump in her throat.

Newspaper clichés, Brett had called them, and that was exactly right. Maybe his contempt was entirely justified?

'Janey?'

'I'm here.' She swallowed back the urge to cry.

'It sounds good. But I thought you were coming straight back? You said you'd be writing it here.'

'I had an accident. My car's in the garage.'

'Nothing serious, I hope.' He didn't pause for an answer. Phones were ringing all round him. 'What's your hotel, if there are any queries?'

'I'm not at a hotel——' she paused, dreading the

response she knew her reply would prompt '—I'm staying at Brett Britain's house. There wasn't a hotel room free.'

'Oh yes?' Reg leered almost visibly into the phone. 'Tell that to the Marines! Well, love, don't forget to keep your notebook handy—day and night! Maybe we can have a follow-up, "The Real Brett Britain— Late Night Secrets of a Millionaire Recluse" by Janey Goodheart!'

'You're disgusting, Reg.' She said wearily. 'You're also an anachronism. These days men and women quite often share a roof without it meaning a thing. Life's changed, you know. Women don't even wear waspies any more!' Her voice was harsh with sarcasm but he simply chuckled.

'That's my girl! I know you think I'm prehistoric, but there's life in the old fellow yet. You should try me some time.'

The meaningless office banter left a sour taste in her mouth, yet when she put the phone down the oppressive silence seemed to envelop her with fears and fantasies. Her thoughts were pulled back to Brett and the other men on the darkening hills. Surely they couldn't search after dark? Surely she would see Brett one more time before she left?

She switched on the lamps and lit the fire, but although she tried to read all her nerves were straining for the sound of a car engine. Of course, the men might have come off the mountain already, she reasoned. Brett could have decided to stay at the pub, or with a friend. Maybe they had even chosen to bivouac on the mountains, to start searching again at first light.

She knew nothing about how such rescue teams operated, just as she knew nothing of Brett's skills as a climber, or indeed anything about his life at all.

In the flames of the fire she conjured his dark, sensuous profile, his disturbing eyes, the fall of dark hair across his forehead. If anything should happen to him—she went cold. It was impossible! There was too much life in his body, too much vitality.

Yet she had seen death claim her father, and knew its power to wipe out all trace of life from even the strongest of spirits.

Her heart seemed scarcely to beat. A world without Brett, living and breathing, was a world she could not think of. But the wind was howling, driving rain like hammers against the window, and up on the mountains was a treacherous dark that would claim any man who put a foot out of line.

'Come back,' she breathed, willing him safe, 'come back.' And she added silently, hopelessly, 'To me.'

The faintest glimmer of sound interrupted Janey's thoughts. She jumped up. It was a car coming along the coast road. She stood stock still, willing it to slow at the turning. It did. As it laboured down the track to the house she ran to fling open the kitchen door. Light poured out into the wild darkness, framing her slim figure as she stood on the step, and the wind caught at her hair and her clothes.

Out of the darkness came Brett, and her hands went out towards him.

'Thank God you're all right!' Relief flooded her voice.

Tiredly he walked past her and dumped his rucksack on the table.

'We found them at dusk,' he said flatly. 'It was a long haul down. One had a broken ankle.'

He turned and she gasped. He had a bloody gash across one eyebrow.

'What happened? You're hurt.'

'It's nothing. Just a cut from a slate.'

His eyes met hers and when he saw the way she looked at him, her hands still stretched towards him, his expression changed.

'Why——' He stopped. 'Anyone might think you really cared!' His voice was harsh.

'Of course I care. I was so worried——' she cried out, but he cut her off with a scything motion of his hand.

'Why should you be worried? What happens to me means nothing to you. As you said yourself, it's only physical! Just a little torrid lust! Worried!' He spat the word out as if it tasted foul in his mouth. 'The only thing you worry about, Janey, is yourself!'

'Oh!' She pressed her hands to her mouth, terrified by his flood of anger. 'It's not true!'

'Isn't it?' He stepped towards her and grasped her arms. 'I didn't notice you worrying about me when you decided to walk out all those years ago! But then I suppose you'd got what you came for. Had enough. So you decided to leave.'

He was a strong and terrifying figure, his hair thick and tousled, his eyes shadowed with fatigue.

She was shaking in his grip, roused by his closeness. Fear and longing struggled inside her until her head began to swim.

'It wasn't like that——'

'Well, you can save your excuses for later. I've heard all I want to hear from you about the nature of our relationship. And I can certainly do without that worried wifely act of yours. I'm cold and I'm tired and I'm hungry.'

'I can get you something.' Her eyes flickered across the kitchen.

His eyes glittered and his grip tightened on her arms. 'I'm not talking about food. I'm talking about you, this.' Brutally his mouth came down on hers, hard and insistent with naked need.

She tore her head sideways. 'Don't!'

'Why not? You know it's what we both want.' His breathing was harsh.

'I can't.' She struggled in his arms, but he pulled her ruthlessly back against him.

'Why? Wouldn't those "friends" of yours approve?' His voice twisted.

'If you like! It's none of your business!'

Deliberately he tightened his embrace, until she could feel the whole hard length of him against her body.

She turned her face, but her pulses were hammering with desire at his rough passion.

'You have no rights over me,' she got out.

'That depends on how you define it,' said Brett cruelly.

His hand lifted her chin until she was forced to

look at him, and she quailed when she saw the hard glitter of his eyes.

What he read in her own eyes, and in the trembling of her body, made his mouth twist in slow triumph.

Arrogantly he trailed a hand down her neck, down the soft hollow of her collarbone, to possess one breast. She shivered. His cold caress was shamingly exciting. Then his fingers probed the stiffening flesh beneath the cotton of her shirt, his eyes watching her until he bent to kiss her again, with a deep hunger.

This time there was no escape. His mouth possessed her utterly, whirling Janey down into the deep waters of her own pent-up need. Without thought, she began to respond to his demands. Her body pressed to his as he forced her head back and plundered her mouth with his tongue. His hands roughly moulded the long curve of her spine, from the nape of her neck to the swell of her hips, then impatiently opened her shirt to seek the warm curves inside. She shuddered and groaned as his hands probed under the thin silk and lace, peremptorily claiming her as of right.

Brett's hands explored the softness of her skin, circling and teasing, until she ached with need of him and any thoughts of resistance were swamped by the sheeting flood of desire he roused in her.

There was a groan, but she had no idea which one of them made the sound, then Brett was scooping her up, wantonly disarrayed, and carrying her to his room.

Held tight against his chest, she heard the

pounding of his heart and smelled the sweat of his day's exertions, but she opened her eyes abruptly as the cooler air of the bedroom washed her fevered senses.

She saw an alarm clock, a pile of books, the familiar pattern of the bed cover, and she remembered—although not clearly—that this should not be happening.

'No!' she faltered, but there was no conviction in her voice. He laid her on the bed. She saw him towering above her, and in his eyes was no compassion, or tenderness, as he surveyed her half-naked form.

'Do you know what a man thinks of, Janey, when he's out on the cold hills?' he observed coldly. Slowly he sat down and methodically began to undress her as he talked. 'It isn't food and it isn't drink, it's warmth. The warmth of sunshine and dry clothes. The warmth of a hot bath or a hot fire. But most of all the warmth of the embrace of a loving woman.'

His eyes held her mesmerised as he talked. She could not move a muscle in protest as he deliberately removed her trousers and began to push her shirt from her shoulders.

'Out there,' he continued, 'when it's cold and wet and getting dark and you don't know if you're searching for a couple of frightened campers or two rapidly stiffening corpses, you start realising what you would miss most in life if it should be your bad luck to be the one who accidentally steps over a five-hundred-foot drop. And you vow to yourself that if you get home in one piece, then you'll go straight out and get it.'

Her shirt was off now, discarded on the floor. She lay before him clad only in her wisps of pants and bra. Almost casually he traced the curves of her body, but the light stroking of his fingers communicated so much held-back passion that she trembled under his touch.

He stood up and began to pull off his shirt, holding her eyes with his. It was the same broad-shouldered body, the same strong chest with its scattering of dark hair that she remembered so well.

'Of course,' he continued matter-of-factly, 'in my case the loving woman isn't available. So I'll just have to make do with the embrace.'

He came to her again and pulled her roughly up into his arms. The shock of flesh on flesh assaulted her starved senses. Her eyes had drunk in the sight of his body, but now her eyes closed as the smell and touch of him swamped her.

'All I hope,' he said darkly against her hair, 'is that the embrace is as warm as I dreamt of it, up on those hills.' There was an edge of threat in his voice which set her trembling in his arms. 'After all, I know the passion you're capable of, Janey. You can't pretend to me that you're either an innocent virgin or a bloodless ice maiden.'

'All that's in the past! You can't summon passion to order!' she got out. She felt as good as naked, stripped of all protection, and her voice was tinny and high, unconvincing even to herself.

In reply he kissed her briefly, savagely, then stood

up. His hands were at the buckle of his jeans' belt, but he paused. 'All right,' he grated angrily, as she caught her uneven breath, 'I've never yet sunk as low as rape, and I don't much fancy starting now. If, as you say, "all that" is over, then get your clothes and go to another room.'

She started up, hands at her throat. It was a reprieve. She could go. So why did she feel such a draining despair? And why were her feet not carrying her swiftly from the room?

He turned away from her and she stared with bitter helplessness at his back. She was lost, and he knew it, betrayed by her aching need for him. All these years she had longed to hold him in her arms again, and have him gather her close. Oh, she had denied it to herself, buried her feelings beneath such a mountain of work so that at nights she had been too tired to lie awake and dwell on the empty space beside her. But they had always been there, wanting only the slightest spark to flare them ragingly to life again.

Brett said with scorn, 'Remember what they say— He who hesitates is lost. Or should it be she who hesitates——'

Still she could not move. He swung back to her, a harsh look of triumph on his face, and let his eyes rake over her. 'You've had your chance,' he said roughly. 'I hope you're not expecting me to conduct you politely to a spare bed, because my gallantry has definite limits, and those are up.'

She looked at him mutely, imploringly, but for what she did not know.

'I want you, Janey,' he said bluntly, 'and I damn

well can't wait any longer.'

As he spoke he walked over to her and pulled her up into an embrace which brooked no more hesitation and delay. He kissed her roughly, his body hardening into instant desire. She knew then that she was truly lost. She had hesitated, torn by conflicting desires, and in that pause had betrayed not only herself, but, far worse, had betrayed——But she could not keep hold of her thoughts as Brett's kisses shot her through with molten fire. She yielded against him, the hours, days and years of longing flowering into a burning desire that was fuelled by the thrust of his body against hers.

Brett pushed her down and stripped the last garments from her. Then he stood and divested himself of the last of his clothes, his body roused and ready before he was with her again, kissing her lips, his tongue roaming the softness of her mouth. Janey's arms embraced him as he cupped her breasts, burying his head there and she groaned, her hips pushing up to his. His hands explored her waist, the softness of her parting thighs, his fingers tracing again the map of her body, remembering its most secret, vulnerable places.

His caresses were skilful, experienced. She writhed with a mounting need as his mouth tugged at her nipples, and his imperious hands made her long to open to him.

Now his hands were holding her wrists, pinning her arms like a helpless butterfly to the pillows as he moved his body across hers and thrust into her without ceremony.

'Oh!' she cried out.

In the past she had caused him grief and his revenge was to take, now, what he so urgently desired. Yet she gasped in a different way as they were fully one again, man and wife.

He paused, releasing her hands, and began to move strongly inside her, forcing her to an instant thrusting response which took them both on a spiral, up and up, their bodies straining together until pleasure and pain were as mixed as the slick of sweat which mingled on their skins.

'Oh,' he gasped, as with powerful energy he thrust still harder against her, rearing up and dispelling with one last movement of his hips his bursting desire.

As she felt him convulse inside her she, too, was lost in her own passion, straining against him until a flooding bittersweetness left her panting and drained.

Slowly the tempest subsided. Brett moved from her and she felt chilled and exposed. She waited, unmoving, for him to break the silence, but he had turned away, sprawling on the far side of the bed. She waited longer. Finally she raised herself on one elbow, unable to bear the silence any longer. 'Brett?' She saw his beautiful limbs sprawled carelessly across the bed, his profile showing as clear as as carving against the white pillow. His eyes were closed, his breathing was even. He was deeply asleep.

In sleep he looked younger, more vulnerable. At first, she felt a deep stab of rejection, but as she watched him she could see he was a man exhausted.

Hurt was replaced by a piercing knowledge of the depth of her love for him as she gently pulled the covers up over him and lay down again at his side.

Sleep, she was sure, would not come as easily to her. Beyond the undrawn curtains was a glittering moonlit view of silver water and inky black islands. It was as cold and bleak as her thoughts. She loved Brett, but he did not love her back, only desired her. And now he had had what he desired.

What had just happened between them should never have taken place, she knew that, although, with spent desire still rocking her body with waves of contentment, she could not clear her head enough to remember exactly why.

Despite everything it felt right to be here with Brett beside her. Even their angry lovemaking had seemed urgent and necessary. And his deep and even breathing was giving her a strange and misguided sense of security. Slowly her eyelids began to drop and sleep came.

'Janey?' There were fingers tipping her chin round. Her eyes opened to see Brett propped on one elbow, regarding her closely. Joy flooded her, then she remembered.

'Don't,' she said tightly. 'Don't say anything.' She could not bear more of his scorn. She looked away from his close gaze. It was morning.

'I wasn't going to,' Brett said softly, and he reached for her with unexpected tenderness.

This time it was different. This time there was gentleness and restraint. Brett found her lips and kissed her slowly and for a long time, like a thirsty man remembering the taste of water. She moved to him, embracing him closely, as his lips languorously kissed her neck and shoulders. Then he found her lips once more and they were lost to everything except the other's presence and pleasure.

Once he lifted his head and looked at her deeply, with an expression that seemed to speak of wariness and pain. Instinctively she reached to pull him closer. He was her husband and she ached to comfort and protect him. But the moment was fleeting and her body throbbed with rousing delight as he kissed her again and stroked her breasts and the softness of her stomach.

The way he touched her told her he had forgotten nothing of the long nights they had lain together in London. He pulled her against him. 'Touch me,' he groaned, against her hair, and her fingers found the core of his powerful, perfect body, making him move against her touch until they inflamed each other with mounting desire.

Yet he still held back, kissing and caressing every inch of her until she quivered with a white ache of arousal that threatened to spill and flood. Only then, when she lay back, open to him, guiding him with her hands, did he move to possess her and take her slowly to a sensuous fulfilment that rolled over them both like a bursting wave of sweet sensation.

Brett lay with her, unmoving, one hand cupping a breast. Slowly, sensuously, lips reddened by his kisses, she turned on the pillow and opened her eyes. Hazily she began to take in the sweep of his dark lashes, the straightness of his nose and lips, the stubbornness of his chin and a thick claw of panic suddenly raked her heart.

Like father, like son.

The old proverb echoed ringingly in her mind. Brett, lying there, was so exactly like Will as she went to wake him each morning.

Her beautiful son. The light of her existence! How could she have forgotten him so completely, and all the complexities that his secret existence enmeshed her in?

She tossed her head as if in blinding pain. The one vital reason why she should have kept Brett at arm's length, out of her life. The ultimate reason why they should not be lying here in this false intimacy, when hearts could be opened and confessions so easily spilt without a thought.

'Oh, Will!' she breathed. 'I'm so sorry.' The words trembled out unconscious from her agony of shame, barely audible, but Brett heard.

His eyes snapped open, and a look of cold contempt slowly hardened his features. He rolled immediately away from her and levered himself up in the bed.

Horror flooded through her. What on earth had she done? What had she said? How could she have been so stupid?

She braced herself for questions, not knowing what she would say if he quizzed her closely. Would she confess? Would her secret be out for ever?

But there were no questions.

'Poor Will.' The words were snapped out with icy scorn.

'It's not what you think——' Automatically she began to protest. Then she stopped. Better he think her a faithless lover than to suddenly discover she was a betraying mother.

If she were ever going to tell him the truth, then it should not be like this, a secret forced out from unwilling lips.

'Save your breath. Your love life is of no interest to me!'

He flung off the covers and swung out of bed, shrugging on his clothes. Janey told herself she should feel relief at his mistake, but she felt only a chill emptiness as she watched him.

He looked down at her contemptuously. 'In my time,' he said, 'I've met quite a few women who could disassociate their morals from what they chose to do with their bodies. Some of them even made quite a fortune by trading on their skill—after all, if you're not too fussy about who makes love to you, why not turn it into a lucrative trade? What I didn't realise until now was that my wife was one of them!'

She blanched with shock. 'How dare you——'

'Oh, I'm not saying you'd ever sink quite that low. But I must say I'm surprised at the performance you can turn in even when, on your own admission, you don't give a damn about me, and there's obviously someone else who matters in your life.'

She turned away, hanging her head so her tousled hair hid her face. 'You know nothing about my feelings.'

'I know what you've told me,' snapped Brett. 'It's enough.' He reached for his pocket and dropped some car keys on to the bedside table. 'If your car's ready I suggest you take my car to the ferry. I dare say you'll be leaving early.'

'I'll be glad to!'

'I look forward to reading what you write about me—although I don't suppose for one minute that you will tell your readers the real truth about your visit.'

His flaying words sparked sudden resistance in her. Fuelled by anger at his undeserved insults she lifted her head and her eyes flashed violet.

'I'll tell them enough! Enough for them to realise just what sort of man Brett Britain is!'

'And what sort is that—no, don't bother to answer. I'll wait and read it in the gutter press!'

'If that's what you think, then I'll make sure the piece lives up—or should it be down?—to your expectations!'

And she would, Janey vowed silently, as anger and humiliation boiled impotently inside her, a seething cauldron of shame and fury, love and hate.

Brett turned and, with a last look that seemed to strip the very skin from her naked form, strode out.

Alone, she sat among the tangled bedclothes, staring at the view beyond the window until welling tears made the clear outlines of the landscape melt into a running pattern of meaningless colour.

CHAPTER SEVEN

'HELLO?' Put me through to copy, please.'

Janey spoke urgently into the pay phone. All morning, on the long drive south, she had composed angry, vengeful words in her head, polishing phrases in her mind until they glittered with venom.

Professionally, she was proud of the final effect, although her heart felt sick and heavy. But the iron grip of hurt which Brett had inflicted kept her true to her vow. She had alerted the newspaper that a change of copy was on its way and now, shouting into the phone at the motorway service station, she dictated the blistering words.

'Proud . . . vain . . . contemptuous of all who cross him . . .' They fell with distressing ease from her tongue.

'Phew,' said the copy-taker, when she had finished. 'You didn't like him much, did you?'

'No,' she snapped. 'Like' was certainly not a word she could apply to Brett Britain. Hate, maybe. Despise. Love. But not like.

She replaced the receiver and leaned her forehead against the cool wall of the booth.

Love. Yes. She loved Brett, with all her heart. She had always done so, and always would. That was exactly why she felt so sick and wounded now. Bad enough that *anyone* should think what he now thought of her ... But the man you loved? She shuddered. The visit had been a complete disaster. She had been right to dread it, and right, too, to be sure life would never be the same again. Uncomfortable guilt and unassuagable longings penetrated her thoughts at every turn. She felt fearful and uneasy about what the future would hold, now, for herself and Will.

She opened her bag and groped for a tissue. Instead, a picture of Will——Brett's dark hair and eyes in miniature—stared back at her.

She stared for a long moment at the picture. Will was everything to her, yet Brett had never even seen his son, never known the joy of watching him unfurl from a baby to a lively child. She felt an acute pang of guilt at what she had denied him, a pang as biting at the pain his bitter words had caused her earlier.

Well, too bad! She hardened her heart against him, concentrating instead on his unjust, hating taunts. If that was what he thought of her, then it was better—far, far better—for her and Will that Brett stayed out of their lives for ever.

It was late by the time she reached home, and she paused only to kiss Will's innocent sleeping face before climbing wearily into her own bed.

Even so, she was already awake when Will came hurtling into her bed to smother her with rough kisses and tell her all his news, although it was not until much later, when he was busy with his breakfast, that she was able to snatch up the newspaper which lay on the mat and turn to the only page she cared about.

'Brett Britain—the bitterness behind the bestsellers' screamed the headline. There was a hollow-ness of apprehension beneath her ribs as she read on.

'Janey Goodheart meets the world's top novelist and finds that fame and fortune have done little for his character.'

Her palms were pricking with sweat now. Yesterday she had been fuelled by hatred. In the cold light of today she knew she had almost certainly gone too far.

'Brett Britain has always guarded his privacy with jealous care. It is easy to see why. I travelled to Scotland this week, to his island hide-away, to be granted his first-ever national Press interview, and I found a man with arrogance but no warmth, the ability to talk, but not to listen, with such certainty of his own rightness that no other versions of the truth are allowed to intrude on the conclusions he so readily jumps to.' She read on, feeling sick with herself. 'He says he prefers to live alone. One gets the distinct impression that no one is considered good enough to share the Britain hearth and home. But possibly the truth lies elsewhere? That no woman can put up with his unspeakable arrogance for any length of time?'

There was more, much more, until the last damning sentence. 'He has done right to mask his personality for so long. Revealed, it is not a pretty sight.'

Her mouth was dry. Never before had she written a piece that was so ruthlessly wounding. What was worse, the article was unfair, and she knew it. She was deeply ashamed to have allowed herself to write from spite, not professional judgement.

The phone rang. It was Reg, from the office.

'Great piece, Janey! Great. Great. A real stinger! Everyone's talking about it.'

'Thanks,' she said dully. 'I won't be in today. It's my day off.'

'Yes, sure. You're in tomorrow, though. The Old Man's summoned you. Ten o'clock in his office.'

'The Editor?' Her eyes opened. Such summonses were rare, and always about something serious.

'Well, it can't be a libel case—the lawyers went through the piece with a fine tooth-comb. Perhaps it's a rise?'

'Perhaps.' She couldn't laugh with him. She felt so low already that the last thing she felt able to cope with were problems at work.

When Reg rang off she battled to give Will her full attention. It was hard at first, but as the day progressed through its gentle domestic routines, she began to relax. Not for the first time, she thought how wonderful it would be not to have to scurry off to work each day, and have the time to cook and play and simply enjoy her son.

Yet the next day it was back to her office clothes and a crisp, professional manner.

At ten sharp she knocked on the Editor's door.

'Good morning,' he said from behind his enormous desk.

'You wanted to see me.'

'I did indeed. So did my visitor here.'

Janey turned.

'You!' she gasped. A flood of embarrassment flushed her face.

Brett, on the other hand, looked perfectly at ease, relaxed on the leather couch. He wore a dark suit and immaculate white shirt, and looked powerful and strange. His hair was tamed from its gypsy wildness, but still gleamed with copper lights as sunlight filtered into the room.

There was a smile about his lips, but it was not a pleasant one, and the glint in his eyes and the set to his jaw frightened her. He nodded coldly.

'Mr Britain came to see me about your article on him, Janey,' the Editor said smoothly. 'It won't be any great surprise to you that he didn't like it.'

She turned, apprehensive, uncertain how much Brett had revealed. Brett's eyes narrowed as if he was enjoying her discomforture.

The Editor came from behind his desk and indicated she should sit down. He took a seat at the other end of the couch. She sank down reluctantly into a chair, her chin lifted high.

'I have to admit it did seem a little harsh,' he said. 'If I had seen it at proof stage I would have thought twice about letting it run.'

'It went through the lawyers,' she said defensively.

'Of course. But lawyers, as you know, are not infallible, and libel is a notoriously slippery concept.'

She could not look at Brett. 'I wrote what seemed to be the truth at the time.'

'I've already told Mr Britain that you are an experienced journalist and a highly respected member of my staff. If it should come to a fight, then you

will have the full backing of myself and the
company. But having said that, I would still prefer
not to have to face Mr Britain's assembled legal
battalions in court.' He stood up and walked to the
window.

'Forgive me if I'm wrong, Janey,' he continued,
'but there seemed an almost personal prejudice in
your writing. Something about the piece—well, it
didn't ring quite true to me.'

She flushed, her eyes drawn to Brett. He was
smoothing his trouser leg with one hand. Her look
went to the firm brown fingers and a sudden vividly
explicit memory of their lovemaking came to mind.
She jerked her head up, met his eyes and looked
instantly away.

The Editor turned back. 'Mr Britain is not
planning to try and sue us—just yet. He's made a
request which seems entirely reasonable to me, not to
say good for the *Standard*. He says he understands
why you might not have gathered a very good
impression of him during your recent meeting, what
with the upset of your accident and everything, and
he has suggested that you be given, as it were,
another bite at the cherry.'

She looked sharply up at him. She couldn't be sure,
but there seemed to be the merest hint of dry
amusement in his voice. Yet at least it seemed Brett
had taken no skeletons out of the cupboard. And
other than him, Tom Simpson was the only other
person to know her secret, and he was safely on
sabbatical on the other side of the world.

'What does that mean?' she queried sharply.

Brett interrupted. 'I suggested you come and watch the filming of my latest book, down in Dorset, and write about that—and me, if you could bear to tackle such an odious subject again. My only condition would be that you penned something a little less histrionic than the hysterical rubbish which appeared yesterday.'

'I've agreed to the request,' the Editor said firmly.

'If we ran a second piece on everyone we ever criticised, the paper would be as big as a telephone directory,' she protested, appalled at the thought of her torture continuing.

'I think we can make an exception in this case. After all, it will cost you no more than a night in Dorset, and the filming will offer a new angle.'

'A night!'

She looked at Brett with hate. He looked levelly back at her.

'I gather that will give you a chance to talk to the director and the actors over dinner,' the Editor said.

Janey knew she was beaten.

'Very well. When is all this to happen?'

'Tomorrow,' Brett said. 'I've arranged to pick you up here in the morning—I don't want you driving into another ditch.'

Only with great effort did she bite back the angry, childish words that sprang to her throat. Then her mother's thoughts turned instantly to Will. 'I have to make arrangements,' she said. 'I can't accept until that's done.'

Brett's gaze hardened instantly. 'I don't think you realise. You don't have a choice.'

She regarded him furiously. 'Very well, I'll be waiting. But hardly with breathless anticipation. Now if you'll excuse me, I've got work to do.'

CHAPTER EIGHT

'WELL, you're great company!'

'It's hardly a social outing.'

Janey had been thinking about Will. That morning, as she had packed her case, he had put his little arms around her neck and said, 'I don't want you to go away.'

She hadn't wanted to go away, either. She felt tired and battered, and longed to have someone to lean on. Nothing had been the same since Brett had summoned her to Scotland.

'Even so, a few pleasantries wouldn't come amiss.'

'I don't feel pleasant!' she hissed. 'I don't want to be here, and you know it.'

Brett had seemed in fine good humour as they drove out of London and through the lush green countryside. He had lowered the top of the car and the wind tousled his hair and made him look young and carefree. But now there was steel in his voice. 'Well, you've only yourself to blame. That article was poisonously unfair—and you know it.'

She tossed her head. 'You could have sued.'

'Legal battles don't interest me. To be honest, I couldn't be bothered.'

'So you had to bother me, instead. Dragging me off on some flimsy pretext——'

'It's not a pretext, far from it.' He looked across at

her. 'I was hurt when I read your piece. Very hurt. And I don't mind admitting it.'

She was startled into meeting his eyes. His words turned a knife beneath her ribs. She had written it to hurt, but had never thought he would let what he considered mere newspaper drivel touch him. Now she knew she had hit her target, she had an overwhelming urge to put out her hand, touch his shoulder, beg him to believe she had not meant a word of it.

Instead she laced her fingers tightly in her lap.

'I don't give a damn what the several million readers of the *Standard* think about me, but I do care what your opinion is. The loathing dripping out of your pen was rather too much to bear.'

'You can hardly be surprised—after what happened, the things you said——'

He drove in silence for some moments. The countryside was unbelievably beautiful in its full summer lushness, but she could take no joy in the rich hedgerows and ripening fields.

'What about Will?' he asked abruptly. 'Did you tell him?'

Her head whipped round to read his profile. He turned to meet her terrified look with a level gaze. 'I thought maybe you had one of those open relationships where everyone confesses everything to everybody.'

She had a nervous urge to laugh with relief that her secret was still safe. 'No, of course not.'

'Does he even know we are married?'

'No, he doesn't.'

Brett drove on in silence. Then he said casually, 'I can see our marriage was a very brief interlude in a crowded life. My heart goes out to poor, wretched Will, if he's going to be thrust aside as readily when his time comes.'

She took a deep breath, then said angrily, 'You seem intent on misunderstanding everything! It wasn't a bit like that, although I don't see any point in going over the old ground of our past yet again! As for Will—no, he'll never be, as you put it, thrust aside! Not *ever*!'

The vehemence of her tone surprised even herself. Brett was silenced, and said nothing for a long time after her outburst, and when he finally did speak it was in the neutral, conversational tone of a stranger. 'I think we should stop for lunch. There's a pub a few miles on that does a good lunch.'

'Whatever you say.'

She went to the cloakroom when they arrived, and by the time she had lingered over the minimal task of brushing her hair and repairing her make-up, Brett was waiting at a table in the window with a bottle of chilled white wine.

He poured her a glass, then said, surprisingly, 'Janey, I've been thinking. I owe you an apology, I shouldn't have said the things I did. I felt somewhat stressed at the time—but that was no excuse.' His tone was cool, but even.

She set down her glass, searching his eyes for some hidden undercurrent of scorn or malice. When she said nothing, Brett continued, 'I don't think we should go on sniping at each other like this. I'm offering a white flag. We've both got work to do on this trip. When it's over, we can go our own ways and never bother each other again.'

His voice was impersonal, almost flat. It was as if he had decided to relinquish a tedious battle, and she did not know how to react, whether to feel relieved or wretched.

'I suppose, then, I ought to apologise as well,' she said grudgingly. 'I had no right to write the things I did. It was done out of pure revenge.'

He smiled at her enchantingly, reminding her vividly of the young writer she had first met.

'I guess we're about as bad as each other. Shall we order?'

Beyond the window dahlias and roses flowered in a rambling English garden, their scent wafting through the open door of the dining-room. To her astonishment she found herself relaxing in Brett's company in a way that had never been possible in their bleak and violent encounter in Scotland.

'They've filmed most of your books, haven't they?' she asked him over coffee. 'Do you always get involved?'

He shook his head. 'I usually have a hand in the script, but that's all. The film world isn't one I relish. Too much waiting around for things to happen. Too many prima donnas thinking they are the only ones that matter. I'd rather sit on Mull, looking out at my islands and bashing those typewriter keys.'

'You love that house very much, don't you?'

Her blue eyes rested on him, open and unguarded. He was the handsomest man she had ever known, she thought, but she had no means of knowing what he thought as he returned her gaze with his own thoughtful stare.

'I do. I need to live near water. In California I've got a house right on the beach. I sit out on the deck at nights, with a tequila at my elbow, and watch the sun go down over the Pacific, vivid red—from the pollution.' He grinned. 'But for real peace of mind give me those silver lochs and dark mountains any day.'

'It is beautiful,' she agreed. 'So solid and snug, and so much space. Children would love it.'

In her mind's eye she saw Will, running and skipping, scrambling up the mountainside or helping haul the dinghy from the barn. Brett was there as well. The loving, attentive father he would never be. Or never be allowed to be? her guilty mind questioned.

'But you've never wanted them?' She hadn't known she was going to say that, but in their peaceful new intimacy it seemed suddenly possible to tread such treacherous ground without danger.

'On the contrary, I'd like them very much. But the right circumstances have simply never arisen.'

'Oh.' She looked down, playing with the stem of her glass.

'What about you?' Her eyes flew back up to his. 'Although I suppose children don't figure in the general scheme of things for high-flying female journalists?'

'Look,' she protested, 'I know that's how you see me. And I know that what I've done lately—the way

I've behaved—must seem to confirm all your prejudices, but I'm not nearly as hard-boiled as you seem to think. I'm only as tough as I have to be to hold down the job. Beyond that I'm not particularly ambitious, or ruthless, or thick-skinned. I wasn't even looking to get into Fleet Street. It was a sheer stroke of luck that it happened at all. I could just have easily still been a small town reporter, living quietly in the Cotswolds——'

He shook his head forcefully. 'Oh no, Janey, never. Even when I first met you it was clear you were destined to swim in a bigger pond. But I have to confess there's something about you now that doesn't add up. If you were a character in one of my books I'd say there was something missing, a piece of the background jigsaw that needed to be slotted into place. When we first met you seemed so innocent and open, too much so for your own good in many ways. I knew when you fled from my flat that day that you were too young for what you had got into, that you had to be left to find your own feet in the world. But now——' he shook his head again, in genuine puzzlement, '—you seem to have grown up too far. I don't know what's happened to you in the last few years, but whatever it is has made you hard and shuttered in a way I never thought you would be.'

'Maybe I've just learnt caution! And maybe it's just with you,' she countered, stung despite the even tenor of his tone. 'After all, our history doesn't exactly lend itself to trusting friendship, does it? You're right I was too young—and I certainly never should have come rushing down to London in the first place—but there were faults on both sides. I wonder if you ever stopped to think how it felt to be marooned in your flat all day, without a job, or friends? I began to feel that the only place you really wanted me was in your bed!'

Brett pushed a hand through his hair. 'I suppose the truth is that I was pretty immature as well,' he conceded. 'So much was happening to me then, on so many different fronts, that I didn't give much thought to anyone but myself. I know now that you can't put people on the back burner until you decide you've got time for them, but at that time life was looking so good that I think I believed I could behave in any way I liked and get away with it.'

She looked at him, knowing he was speaking the truth. 'But why bother with marriage? Our lives would be simpler now without it.'

He raised a shoulder, half shrugging away her question. 'Why do we ever do anything? I suppose one reason was your extreme youth—I felt very responsible for what had happened between us.' His lips closed firmly, as if forbidding any further probing on the point. Then he smiled at her. 'Perhaps I still do,' he added, lightly. 'Perhaps that's why I wanted to see you again, to make sure you were all right—although now I have I can see that you're more than capable of surviving without any help from me.'

Reluctantly she found herself returning his smile, although there was an edge of bitterness in her voice when she spoke. 'I didn't want to see you,' she told him honestly. 'I really and truly didn't. I pleaded with the paper not to send me. I knew it would cause trouble, and it has.'

Briefly he put a hand out and covered hers where it rested on the table.

'We'll both survive,' he said, 'one way or another. After all, we've only got to get through today and tomorrow, then we can both turn our backs and get on with our separate lives again. We've done it before, so I guess we can do it again.'

His fingers squeezed hers, and for a second his gaze was dark behind his smile, but the the waiter came. The moment was gone, and their conversation turned to lighter things.

Getting through, as Brett termed it, was all made far easier, she reflected later, by his total change of mood. He seemed determined to maintain an air of pleasant detachment in spite of their lunch-time exchanges, and distracted her thoughts with diverting conversation for the rest of the drive.

The film set, when they finally reached it, was a beautiful Georgian manor. Brett was greeted as a celebrity as they made their way through the crowds of technicians, and once he had made sure Janey was meeting all the necessary people he disappeared from view.

The director took a break from work to brief her about the day's shooting, and after that she wandered off, chatting idly with the crew members as lights were set up in an elegant panelled library.

All her professional instincts were alert and observant. She was determined to make this article one of her best, to compensate in some way for the childish malice of her last.

When silence was called for she watched carefully while the two leading actors took their place under the arc lights.

Steven Steelman she recognised immediately as one of the country's leading actors. Like Brett he had dark eyes and thick dark hair, but there the similarity ended. To her biased eyes he looked as bland and uninteresting as any even-featured shop window dummy.

Automatically her eyes searched for Brett, to make the comparison. She eventually spotted him in the shadows on the far side of the room, his eyes on the leading lady, in warm appreciation.

Janey followed his gaze. Lynne Manners had a pre-Raphaelite cloud of honey curls which floated about her white shoulders like spun gold. Her eyes were a clear green, and her high cheekbones haughty and exquisite.

She felt a wrench of primitive jealousy, and when the lights were switched off and she saw Steven making purposefully towards her, she found herself greeting him with an enchanting smile which she dearly hoped would be visible across the room.

'They told me the Press was here this afternoon. I hope we're all making a good impression?'

His teeth were so dazzling that she wondered if they were real. 'I thought you were very good just now, but I'm really here to write about Brett Britain.'

'Then put in that he's a wizard with words. I've never had lines which are so convincing.'

She laughed and fished out her notebook. 'I'll

quote you on that, if you don't mind. Have you read
many of his books?'

'I'm not much of a reader. To be honest, I prefer to
relax over a good meal. Which reminds me, I've been
delegated to run you over to the hotel. The Angel.
It's blissful. A real piece of Olde Englande.'

'Oh?' Her eyes flew to Brett, but he was engrossed
with Lynne Manners. Steven followed her look.

'I've already put your case in my car. Brett said he
might be busy here for some time.'

She saw Lynne's slender fingers resting on Brett's
arm. I bet, she thought savagely, and was frightened
by the violence of the feelings that surged within her.

Later she lay on her bed in the ancient inn and
tried to think about the article she would write. But
the memory of that intimate twosome invaded all her
thoughts.

Next door she heard a key turn in a lock and heavy
male footsteps walk across the uneven boards. She
wondered if it was Brett.

The Angel was the retreat of the director and the
stars, she had discovered earlier, and she understood
why when she read the price list and saw her room.

It was exquisitely furnished with polished beech
antiques, and the chintz drapes about the antique
four-poster matched the curtains and cushions. She
turned her head and looked at the empty pillow
beside her, and thought of Brett with longing. This
was not a bed to sleep in alone. At home she was
usually too tired to dwell on thoughts of love, and her
functional single bed inspired no fantasies. But this
bed was the stuff of which dreams were made, she

thought, as she tugged a cord and the heavy curtains fell down into place, turning the bed into a private world, whose soft coverings were gently perfumed by the pots of pot-pourri that stood about the room.

No doubt Brett also had just such a bed, and Lynne Manners—— Stop it! she forced herself. Instead she thought about lunch, and the curious harmony that had flowed from their mutual apologies. Brett had seemed so natural, warm and human, that it was impossible not to see what a loving father he could be to Will. As for Will himself, he was growing fast, beginning to climb trees and kick a ball about the lawn. How could she ever meet his needs as he blossomed into manhood?

Janey sat up, facing again the uncomfortable truths that invaded her thoughts. She had to find a way of confessing the truth to Brett, and the strength to ride out his anger and recriminations. For his sake, and for Will's.

But she also knew she couldn't. Her own longing and love for him made her too weak, too vulnerable. Until she mastered her emotions, she simply could not face what such a confession must bring in its wake.

The shrill of her bedside phone broke into her jumbled thoughts. It was Steven, urging her to hurry, as dinner was about to start.

Relieved to have an excuse to shelve again the impossible problem, she shrugged on a black dress that was high at her throat, but left her slender arms bare, and hastily did her face and hair, before hurrying down to the bar.

It was obvious that the party had been drinking for some time. Steven indicated a seat next to him and fetched her a drink. She met the film's producer and chief cameraman and one or two others, but of Lynne and Brett there was no sign.

There was no sign later when they moved to the dining-room, and the meal was already being served by the time the latecomers arrived. She looked up from her plate at the sound of greetings and was startled to meet Brett's look head on. But her heart froze at the cool indifference of his gaze, more numbing and hateful than any look of hostility or anger. She shivered.

Lynne Manners, at his side, looked every bit as glamorous as she had known she would. She wore a figure-hugging sheath of green, shot through with gold, and her hair was piled high with gold combs. Brett touched her waist casually as he guided her to her seat, and the light contact went through her like a barb of pain.

Recklessly she downed her wine and turned with a glowing smile to Steven. The actor needed little encouragement. He bent close to her as he talked, and slowly one arm eased out across the back of her chair. When his eyes looked intently into hers, she held his look lingeringly.

Once or twice she darted covert looks at Brett, but he showed no awareness of her presence. Only once did she see him regarding the pair of them, and then his gaze held no obvious emotion.

Lynne leant across the table. Janey could see she, too, had been drinking before dinner.

'I hope this is an "off the record" dinner,' she said with a sharp peal of laughter. 'I wouldn't like to see all our little indiscretions misquoted in tomorrow's gossip columns.'

She tipped her head, feeling on familiar ground. She was well used to handling criticism of the Press.

'I don't write gossip. In fact, I very rarely write about the entertainment industry at all. I prefer meatier subjects.'

Lynne's eyes were beady, despite her smile. 'Isn't this meaty enough for you? The country's leading producer, director, actor——'

'And actress,' Steven put in gallantly. She blew him a kiss.

'It's an impressive gathering. But I'm here to write about Brett. The filming is just a peg to hang the story on. My main interest is how easily the book turns into a film.'

'It's as easy as pie,' said the director. 'The story works like a dream and all the characters are completely rounded. I predict it's going to be the box-office hit of the decade, and thanks to Brett here, we're all going to be immensely rich.' He lifted his glass in a joking toast, which Brett acknowledged with an easy grin.

'So we'll hardly figure in your article?' Lynne said to Janey. Her voice was hard. 'Well, I must say that's a relief. As far as I can see, reporters never get anything right.'

Janey smiled sweetly. 'Sometimes it can be quite difficult. Especially if people insist on telling lies.' Her eyes held Lynne's. 'For instance, you wouldn't believe the number of people who tell us they're younger than they are.' The barb went home. Lynne flushed and turned away. Janey looked at Brett and a small quirk played around his lips. For a brief second a private current passed between them, shafting her through with instant quivering desire. To cover her confusion, she took out her notebook and asked the producer the last few final questions that would wrap up her article.

The dinner stretched on, with port following the cheese and the haze of laughter and cigar smoke growing thicker around the table. Steven talked relentlessly to her, bending ever closer as the level in his glass sank, and was filled, and sank again.

'I'm sorry?' she said, when she realised he had at last paused for a response. Her eyelids were drooping. Will had woken her up at six that morning. He repeated his remark, but her ears were buzzing with tiredness. 'I'm sorry, I'm afraid you'll have to excuse me. I'm very tired. I think I'll just slip away.' She stood up, nodded to the assembled party, and headed swiftly for the door.

To get to the bedrooms she had to cross a small stableyard, and she paused to drink in the fresh summer air. A full harvest moon hung behind the heavy leaves of a sweet chestnut and she gazed up at it, longing to soothe her inflamed feelings in its remote beauty.

Then there was a step, a figure at her side, a hand on her bare elbow. Her heart hammered. She turned, eyes wide, lips parted, pulses racing.

'It's lovely out here, but you'll catch your death

without a wrap. I've got a bottle of best brandy in my room that will warm you up.'

Janey's heart dropped so savagely that she thought it would splash and spill on the cobblestones. Steven, swaying slightly, stood at her side.

She shook her head. 'Thank you, Steven, but I really do want to go to bed—alone,' she added, with a laugh to soften the rejection.

'You disappoint me!' he said, 'I rather thought earlier——' She felt a pang of remorse at having used him so ruthlessly.

'You're a very attractive man,' she told him. 'And I'm flattered by the offer. But you see,' she paused, 'I'm married.'

The words hung in the air. She hadn't said that to anyone for years, but even as she spoke them, she realised they rang with solid, unassailable truth. She was married irrevocably to Brett. He had captured her, heart, mind and body, all those years ago, and she would never break free from those bonds.

'Aha!' She could tell his disapointment was merely fleeting. 'Lucky man. I suppose there's no point in trying to persuade you that I'm here, and he's not, and what the eye doesn't see——'

She shook her head, her lips twisting with irony at his words. What would he think if he knew her husband had sat across the table from them at dinner tonight?

'In that case, my lovely, I'll leave you to your chilly musings and go to my loveless cot——' With a dramatic hand to his forehead, he wove off into the darkness.

She stood unmoving, the jealousy she had been holding at bay all evening suddenly sweeping over her in such a wash of flaming hatred, that her hands shook and her nails gouged her palms as she pressed her fingers into tight fists.

All night she had sat smiling sweetly at Steven while Lynne made open play for Brett, and he returned her obvious interest. She had seen her hand on his arm and his hand at her waist, and later, she was certain, those casual touches would lead to other, far greater intimacies.

Her breath caught in her throat like a cry as she thought of his strong hands exploring that porcelain flesh, of his fingers tangling in those honey curls. She knew all too well the rhythms of his lovemaking, the groans that would escape his lips in the final moments, and her whole being cried out against it.

She bit her lip, hard, trying to bring herself to reason. Brett had no place in her life. Her life was Will, only Will, and their life together. Vainly she struggled to bring the little boy to mind. She could see his childish, eager face as plainly as ever, but he was distant and remote from the passions that now surged inside her.

With a sudden blinding flash of clarity she realised that a child, no matter how greatly you loved it, could never be the whole reason for living, should never be. There were adult passions, adult emotions, that demanded fulfilment, and to exclude these, to block them out and pretend they didn't matter, was to live a life of such narrow repression that it could only harm those who had contact with it.

Will was the centre of her universe, and always would be, but to make him that to the exclusion of all else could only be to do him ultimate damage.

She swallowed, alarmed at what she had suddenly understood so clearly. The thoughts had passed through her head in an instant, yet she knew they signalled a deep shift in herself, a new understanding, that would live on long after fevered late-night emotions were calmed.

She began to walk slowly to her room, her heels on the cobbles beating a tattoo which sounded, Brett, Brett, Brett.

He had looked at her so coolly tonight, yet only days ago he had been pressing her down in his bed with an urgency that brooked no hesitation. What had happened?

She felt like a wild woman, primitive and unrestrained. Brett was her man, she thought fiercely. He had always been, right from that first day. Lynne Manners had no right, no right at all! Not even for a night, an hour, a moment!

The hallway was deserted and quiet. She mounted the stairs towards her room, forcing one foot in front of another, wanting to gain the sanctuary of her room before her jealousy prompted her to any wild acts. With heightened awareness, she felt the polished wood of the banister under her hand, and saw the rich red of the carpet under her feet. She gained her door, felt for her key.

Then she heard voices, a measured male tone and a light, stagey laugh. She froze, turning. At the end of the corridor, Lynne and Brett came into view. His hand was on her elbow, and they were both far too absorbed to notice her.

'I think,' Brett was saying, 'that if you're supposed to be on set at dawn tomorrow, you ought to get some sleep.'

'Sleep! I barely need it. I like to burn the candle at both ends—and make-up can easily deal with any bags under my eyes.'

'But what about my film?' Janey knew from his bantering tone that there would be smile creases at his eyes. 'I don't want you turning in a lousy performance, just because of the wild nightlife of west Dorset!'

Lynne's voice was sultry in reply. 'Who said anything about a lousy performance?' The innuendo was unmasked. 'I've got a bottle of champagne in my room, maybe we could crack it and have an in-depth discussion of my performance.'

Brett said, 'I think I've had enough tonight—to drink, that is.'

It was like being in a nightmare. She didn't want to hear, but she couldn't stop. She didn't want to be there, but she couldn't move.

Stop it! she screamed at them silently. Stop it! Stop it! Stop it!

Suddenly there was an echo of sound ringing around the quiet corridor. She saw Lynne and Brett both turn, startled, towards her. To her utter horror she realised she must have shouted aloud. The dying reverberations were all around them. Lynne looked furious. Brett seemed merely amused.

'I'm sorry?' Lynne snapped. 'Did you say something?'

'I suppose I must have done,' she snapped back. Reviving anger and jealousy coursed, with the wine, through her veins, unleashing her tongue.

'I can't see our conversation has anything to do with you!'

Janey saw Lynne's hands still held Brett's elbows. Something finally snapped. She dashed her bag to the floor and ran forward, pulling the actress from him. 'Don't! Leave him alone!'

Lynne elaborately raised her eyebrows.

'I think our little reporter here has had too much to drink, don't you?' she said to Brett. 'And she seems to have developed a rather touching crush on you. Perhaps we should be charitable, and help her to her room?'

Janey whirled round to face her. 'I'm a great deal more sober than you. Sober enough not to be out looking for one-night stands with married men!'

Lynne's eyes opened in cynical disbelief. 'Married! So what? Aren't we all?' She shook her head, then light seemed to dawn. 'Or is the wife a chum of yours? Is it sisterhood time? You're keeping her property safe in the hope that she'll do the same for you some day?' She turned to Brett, looking up at him under her lashes and reclaiming his arm.

Janey could not look at Brett. But she sensed his presence, watching, waiting. She trembled with fury. It was all she could do not to slap the star across her china face.

'Oh, his wife is a very good friend of mine!' Her

voice was shaking with anger. She did not know what she was going to say, and she did not care. 'I know her very well indeed! In fact you could say I know her as well as I know myself!' From the corner of her burning blue eyes she saw Brett begin to smile. She knew with blinding clarity that she was on the edge of a precipice. There was still time to step back. But if she went on, that was it. No more hiding, no more safety.

Lynne suddenly exploded in anger. 'I don't give a damn! Come on, Brett. We don't need this.'

'*I'm* his wife!'

It was said. Even as she uttered the words she felt her anger drain away from her. Lynne dropped her hand from Brett's arm instantly. The shock of Janey's words left her face doll-like with surprise. 'I see,' she said stiffly. 'I had no idea.'

Janey felt a hollow, sick emptiness creeping beneath her ribs. Still she could not look at Brett, but kept her chin up, meeting Lynne's startled eyes.

'I really had no idea,' Lynne repeated. 'You didn't seem——'

'——like an old married couple.' Brett put in. She finally turned to look at him. There was an air of amusement about him, but also a darker, dangerous look in his eyes that made her shiver with apprehension. She dropped her gaze.

Lynne was not a top actress for nothing. She quickly regained her poise. 'I think, if you'll excuse me, I'll make my excuses and leave. I suddenly find I'm rather tired, after all.' She turned and swayed slowly away down the corridor, her dress gleaming

over the slim outline of her perfect figure. Brett
watched her go, not bothering to hide the attraction
the sight held for him.

She felt blank, sick, and frightened. And Brett was
an unknown quantity beside her. She had no idea
what would happen now.

CHAPTER NINE

BRETT took the key from her nerveless fingers and ushered her into the room closing the door behind them.

Then he leant against the back of the door, loosened his tie and set his hands on his hips, waiting.

When Janey stood silent, head bowed, he finally said, 'Well, what was all that about?'

She shook her head, confused, the anger entirely gone from her.

He took off his tie and undid the neck of his shirt with deliberate, casual gestures. 'Just the malicious desire to rob me of what looked to be a very promising night of pleasure?' There was a tone in his voice that unsettled her. He didn't seem angry, more amused, even triumphant.

'I'm sorry, I don't know what came over me,' she whispered. She stepped forward, away from him, and put out a hand to the post of the four-poster bed for support, feeling sick and ashamed. Then Brett was behind her, sliding his hands around her waist, pulling her back against him.

'Perhaps,' he said against her ear. 'You just didn't like the thought of others having a good time, while you went to your cold sheets alone?'

'If I'd wanted someone to warm my bed, I'd have taken up Steven Steelman's offer,' she said tightly.

'I see.' His arms tightened about her waist. 'Then I can only flatter myself that it was jealousy.'

She said nothing. He turned her to face him.

'You were jealous,' he insisted, tipping her chin so she had to meet his eyes.

'All right!' she burst out. 'Yes. Yes. I was! I was stupid. I had no right to break in like that! What you do is no business of mine.'

At her words a lazy smile of triumph creased his features.

'It really doesn't matter a damn. I'd far rather be in your bed than hers. I'm just curious, Janey. I don't understand why, when I'd decided to do the decent thing and give you the clear berth you'd been pleading for, you suddenly decide to claim your marital rights.'

As he spoke his hands were at her neck, moving up over the soft skin under her hair to hold her head. She saw the straight brows that echoed the firm, sensual strength of his lips, the glossy hair, the squareness of his jaw, and the lines that humour and pain had etched lightly at his eye. His gaze was intense, direct, reaching down to her innermost depths, stirring her deeply.

'I don't know, either,' she muttered, unable to hold his look. His closeness, his unhidden desire for her was filling her with longing, blurring her senses with a throb of need.

But she wanted him as more than a lover. She wanted him as husband, father, friend. History had already taught her that lesson. Whereas he wanted

her in the only way he had always wanted her—in his
bed.

Now his hands were moving lower, slowly parting
the zip of her dress, exploring the soft skin of her back.
She felt as if she were melting inside, aquiver with
sensation. For a moment she allowed her forehead to
rest weakly against his chest.

But there was Will. Always Will to think of.

'Don't,' she got out. Instead he laid his lips against
her ear and neck, giving her small, biting kisses that
hinted of insistence.

'I said, don't.'

She heard a sharp intake of breath.

'Janey, I'm getting very tired of your games.' There
was steel in his voice, and his hands slid lower down
the curves of her hips. She caught at his arms, feeling
the bones beneath the skin.

'You mustn't!'

'Why not?'

She shook her head in confusion.

'Isn't this what you wanted, when you staged your
shouting act in the corridor just now?'

'I don't know what I wanted! I wasn't
thinking——'

With a single angry movement his hands came up
to break her grasp. His look was black with frustrated
anger.

'You,' he ground out, 'have just laid public claim to
your rights as my wife! Now, Janey Britain——' he
laid deliberate emphasis on the name she still held but
never used, '——I have every intention of claiming
mine as your husband.' He gestured angrily towards

the bed. 'That is where I intend to sleep tonight, and not alone, either. And quite frankly I no longer care whether it's with or without your active co-operation!'

'I thought you never sank to rape!'

His eyes narrowed. 'Oh, no,' he said, with dangerous softness, 'with us it would never be that. Your mind might try to push me away, but your body wants me every bit as much as mine wants you. Look what you do to me——' With a grip like iron he grasped her wrist and pulled her hand to him, his need of her. She looked up at him, eyes wide. Then he was pulling her close against him in an insistent embrace. 'It's always been that way with us, hasn't it? You drive me crazy with desire. Just being in the same room as you is a torment. Tonight at dinner——'

'Tonight at dinner you only had eyes for Lynne Manners!' The childish pique was out before she could bite it back.

'No.' The word came out curt and crisp. 'Maybe it looked like that, but it was second best. It's you I want, Janey. All of you, as loving and yielding as I know you to be.'

She hesitated and his arms tightened harder about her.

'I can't,' she cried, her eyes on his, willing him to understand. 'I can't, Brett. There's no future for us, there are reasons. You don't understand. Good reasons.'

'Like Will, I suppose,' he said harshly.

She nodded. His look darkened to black thunder. 'Get rid of him!'

'I can't. It's not like that!'

His breath exploded in anger. 'To hell with Will!' He dismissed her presumed lover with a slash of his hand. A glaze of colour heightened his cheekbones, and made his eyes bright. Abruptly he kissed her, harsh and hard.

'Hold me,' he commanded.

Her arms went woodenly round him.

'Not like that!' he growled, and he kissed her again, opening her mouth and plundering its soft secrets. Her body ached for him, but she held herself unmoving against his assault.

He drew back and scrutinised her. She tossed her head and managed to hold his gaze.

'Why—I've really had enough. Janey!' He pulled her hard against him, her hips to his, so his desire was inflamed further.

A small gasp escaped her, and the sound broke his final restraint. With one brute gesture he ripped her dress from zip to hem and tossed it aside. He picked her up and threw her on the bed, kissing her savagely and tearing away her bra so his hands could circle and torment her aching breasts.

'Oh!' He made her writhe and gasp with the forcefulness of his need, and shafts of pleasure winged through her as his lips caught her nipples. Urgently his hands pushed away the last of her clothing, so she lay naked and spread beneath him.

She turned her head on the cover as he reared back to watch her face as his fingers teased and probed those intimate curves that only he had ever known.

Blurred against her eyes, through the spread fire of

her hair, were the delicate flowers of chintz, so absurdly out of key with their desperate passion. Then her eyes closed as she felt his lips on the softness of her stomach and thighs, the feelings he was conjuring in her almost too much to bear.

She arched from the bed, reaching for him, lost now in the wild vortex of love and pain that bound them so inextricably together, but he held himself back from her hands, still clothed, intent only on rousing her beyond reason, exacting vengeance for her earlier coldness.

'Brett!' That was her voice crying out in urgent need. She twisted from his punishing lips and knelt up on the bed, her hair in wild disarray, her lips reddened. 'Please!' Her hands sought his shoulders, holding him, pulling her to him.

His eyes raked over her, taking in her naked, abandoned beauty. His breath was ragged. 'Please what, Janey?' His voice was low and rough, and sent waves of renewed desire coursing through her. Her eyes locked with his in a look that was stripped of all pretence, and sent a shaft of bittersweet love piercing through to her heart. She paused, uncaring that all her great need and longing for him was written openly across her.

'Make love to me,' she heard herself whisper, as his lips sank to hers in a kiss that seemed as long as time and as complex as the universe.

When he raised his head, his voice was shaking with desire.

'No,' he said slowly. '*You* make love to *me*.'

Now it was her hands that undid buttons and thrust

aside clothing, remembering the familiar broad strength of his shoulders, the rough hairs of his powerful chest. His body was roused, but her hands moved to claim him further, his lean hips and unhidden desire.

He lay back on the bed, pulling her down on to him, her head between his hands, and when she kissed him she felt the same mingled need and anger that he had earlier shown her. She loved him so much, but he had caused her so much pain! All the bitterness of betrayal was in the way her lips searched and tormented him until he groaned her name, thrusting up hard against her.

His voice made her open her eyes. Her hair hung down like a curtain, enclosing them in a private world. He breathed roughly, his lips parted, as he, too, opened his eyes. Their gaze was like the calm eye of the storm, a moment of such deep and private emotion, that she knew with sudden certainty that whatever happened between them now, their need for each other would mingle for the rest of their lives.

Then he groaned and moved against her, taking her hips to guide her towards the union for which they both strained.

She cried out as she felt him fill her, complete her, and with a swift movement he turned with her until she was against the master, taking her in an urgent, mounting, whirling ascent to the highest point of passion from which she was suddenly tumbling and falling, gasping and clinging to him as wave after wave of release washed over her, and from somewhere far distant she heard him cry out, and pull her up to him as if he would crush her to him for ever.

When finally he collapsed against her they lay together unmoving. Slowly her senses restored the world to order. She felt the weight of his body half across hers, and became aware of their legs, still entwined. His head lay cradled at her shoulder, his thick hair against her cheek, his breath still uneven on her cheek.

She opened her eyes, feeling completely sated. Ripples of pleasure still spread through her. She wanted the moment never to end.

But it did. Brett rolled on to his back, opened his eyes, and surveyed the magnificent antique four-poster with its elaborate curtains and frilled draperies.

'My,' he said lightly. 'At last we've found a setting baroque enough to match what seems to happen every time you or I cross paths.'

'Don't,' she said urgently. She could not bear the denigration of their lovemaking. Her eyes went over the flounces and tasselled cords. One tug and the draperies would fall around them to shut out the world. If only life were so simple, she thought achingly.

He turned his head to look at her, and with one hand stroked back a curl from her cheek. 'I wasn't going to,' he said gently, 'only I told you once before—I always get flippant when I'm frightened.'

'Frightened?'

'Of this, us.' he gestured at the bed. 'This powerful chemistry between us, Janey—I'm not sure if it's a curse or a blessing.'

'What do you mean?' She found she was whispering

in the intense privacy of the moment. He levered himself on to a elbow and looked down at her.

'I mean I've never found any woman as exciting as you. I've never known anyone I've wanted to make love to so urgently, and so often. I've only got to see you across a room and I want to walk over and take you in my arms. Tonight was purgatory, watching that idiot Steelman breathing all over you, having to pretend I didn't want to get up and punch him on the nose——'

'It was the same for me,' she confessed. 'Watching you with Lynne Manners!'

His mouth crooked enigmatically. 'But this need we have for each other,' he went on, 'it seems to get in the way of everything else. It makes you angry, and me frustrated, and it never leaves us any time to talk, or space to simply enjoy being together.'

'You're saying you can't build a relationship on sex alone. That's the mistake we made all those years ago.' Her heart sank. He was telling her what she already knew all too well, that he wanted her in his bed, but nowhere else. 'I know that—it's just as well we're not trying to,' she added bitterly.

'I don't know about that. In the eyes of the world we already have one.' His tone hardened in response to hers. 'Our marriage is hardly likely to stay the quiet piece of history it's been up till now. Lynne Manners is the darling of all the columnists. She's also a woman spurned. She's unlikely to hesitate before picking up the telephone.'

Her eyes met his with alarm.

'After all,' Brett pointed out reasonably, 'you're

quite a well known lady in your own right, and the Press have been dying to pin some scandal on me for years. They can't bear people who refuse to give them interviews.'

He scrutinised her look. 'Not that it bothers me particularly. Unlike you, I don't feel it was a particularly shameful part of my past. There have been plenty of worse things.'

'I'm sure.' Her voice was cold with the icy fear that was beginning to grip her heart. If their marriage was known, then Will's existence would soon be ferretted out by the more energetic diary writers. Ever since she had met Brett again, she had known her quiet world was being rapidly destabilised. Now she had an acute premonition of its imminent collapse.

'Is there anything we could do?'

'Well, I suppose I could go and knock on her door, tell her you were deranged. Maybe I could say you have developed an unhealthy obsession for me which led to wild fantasies about a marriage. I could say that I'd managed to calm you down and called a doctor to sedate you.' He paused. 'Of course, I'd have to go in and apologise profusely for the embarrassment she'd suffered. I'd have to sit and drink her champagne, work hard at thawing her out—and turn in a pretty credible performance between the sheets before begging her—for my sake—to keep mum.'

'Stop it!' The images he was deliberately conjuring up were too much for her to bear. 'There must be some other way!'

Now he pushed himself back up against the pillows and looked directly at her.

'Why exactly are you so worried, Janey? What is it that you've got to hide?' There was a determination in his voice to get the information he wanted.

'Nothing.' She looked away, unable to bear his raking gaze.

'It's Will, isn't it? Always Will!'

Her eyes went back to him.

'Yes. it's Will,' she said quietly.

His eyes scoured her face. She took a breath, gripping the sheets until her knuckles showed white. Now she would tell him she told herself. Now, now! Then it would be finished, an end to all the fears and lies and deception.

And an end to any lingering hope for your relationship, a taunting inner voice whispered, because what will he think of you when he finds out the truth?

She thrust it away. She loved Brett so much she had to give him the gift of his child. That was the only thing that mattered. Her lips parted and she tried to force out words.

'I don't know what you'll think of me when you find out——' It was coming out all wrong. 'It's not like you think.'

Brett, staring hard at her, did little to make it easier. His hair was tousled and his jaw shadowed, dark and stubborn. 'I know that,' he said. 'You've never seemed like a woman in love. What is it, Janey? A sugar-daddy affair? A "marriage" of convenience?'

'Is that what you think of me?' Her voice rose with pain. He flung himself back on to the pillow.

'I don't know what I think of you, Janey. You tie me

in knots. Tonight I almost began to believe you cared about me, about us—but now——' He turned his head and shot her a dark look. 'It's always the same, isn't it?' he said savagely. 'Once you've got what you want you suddenly remember Will!'

'I never forget him!' she cried out. 'He's never out of my thoughts! Will isn't my lover, he's——'

The sentence was never finished. Her words were cut off by the sudden shrilling clamour of the bedside telephone.

CHAPTER TEN

'Miss Goodheart? I'm sorry to disturb you so late, but I have an urgent call for you.'

Janey knelt up, cradling the receiver, her heart immediately racing with fear. Ann's voice came on the line.

'Janey, I'm sorry about this, it's about Will—but don't worry. He's all right.'

'What is it?' She could feel Brett's eyes on her back, but she did not turn.

'He started to run a temperature this afternoon. I thought it was just a cold or something, but he seemed to get worse after he went to sleep. I called Dr Matthews and we managed to cool him down, but she thinks we ought to admit him to St Mary's for observation. He was really quite feverish for a time, and although the worst seems to be over, she still wants a close watch kept on him.'

'What does she think it is?'

'She doesn't really know—probably some kind of virus.'

'What's he like now?'

'Much better. He knows where he is again now. In fact I half suspect he's enjoying all the fuss. But he wants you——'

'I'll come straight back. No. I'll come to the hospital.'

'It will be the Elizabeth Garret Anderson ward, in

the main block on the High Road.'

'Elizabeth Garrett Anderson,' she repeated, committing it to memory. 'Thanks, Ann. Please will you tell him I'll be there as soon as I can?'

She put the phone down and began to scramble into her clothes. Brett said 'What's the matter?'

'Will,' she said shortly. 'He's been taken ill. They're taking him to hospital.' Frantically she looked around for her shoes. 'I've got to get back to London.'

'How?'

She froze, remembering she had no car. 'I'll call a taxi.'

'You won't get one at this time of night, I'll drive you.' He swung out of bed and began to dress.

'I can manage——'

'I wouldn't dream of letting you,' he said crisply, and before she could argue further he had left her with instructions to meet him by the car.

It was a long, anxious drive, during which barely a word was spoken. A sick band of fear clutched at her heart. Ann was not one to panic, so she must have known Will was in a very bad state, and despite her friend's soothing reassurances she longed to set eyes on her son again.

And behind the curtain of anxiety lay other surging half-formed thoughts. Her world, so carefully built up and preserved, was tumbling around her. Soon there would be no more peace, no more privacy. The world would know of her marriage, and everyone would see the personal spite that had fuelled her savage profile of Brett.

It was only a matter of time now before Brett learnt of Will's existence, and when he did so he would undoubtedly despise her for what she had done.

She had no idea how he would behave, but if he tried to take Will from her, then she knew now it was little more than she deserved.

She glanced covertly at him as he sped along the dark highway, loving every curve of his face, every movement of his hands on the wheel, trusting him totally to get her to the hospital as fast as he safely could. When she told him about Will, she thought, she would lose him for ever, but Will would gain a father he would grow to love and be proud of, and the ache in her heart was eased by the certainty that she had finally found the courage to do the right thing.

Brett drove straight to the hospital. She jumped out instantly, bending down to offer hurried thanks. His face was grave and his eyes anxious.

'I hope it's good news,' he said.

'Brett, I——'

'Not now,' he said. 'Whatever it is, it can wait. You've got other things on your plate,' and he slipped the car into gear and drove off just as soon as she shut the door.

Only much later did she realise just how grateful she had been for his quiet, unquestioning help.

Will had been sitting up in bed when she flew through the doors of the ward, a little too bright-eyed and pink-cheeked, but otherwise much as normal.

Yet Dr Matthews, who was still there, told her that his temperature had soared so dramatically that he had been in danger of convulsing, which was why she had suggested admission to hospital.

Janey stayed with him that night, and the next day he continued to make good progress. But the following night his temperature suddenly shot up again and there had been anxious hours before he slipped into a laboured sleep. Only after a further three days of ups and downs did the hospital pronounce him finally on the mend, and she was able to take him home and pick up the threads of her life again.

She felt drained and exhausted, and longed to be able to devote her time to nursing Will back to full strength. But instead she found herself working late at nights to clear the backlog of work on her desk and finish her second piece on Brett in time to meet the deadline.

One evening, as she stepped tiredly out into the street and flagged down a taxi, anxious to get back to Will, a familiar car slowed to a stop at the kerb behind the black London cab. Brett jumped out.

'Janey! Good. I'm glad I've caught you. You left these at the Angel the other night.' He proffered her tape recorder and a bag of make-up. 'There was a black dress, too, but it wasn't in any state to wear again. I threw it out.'

She looked at him sharply, but there was no hint of irony or apology in his voice.

She felt dazed by tiredness and the sudden shock of seeing him again.

'How did you get them?'

'I had to drive back to Dorset. There was some work to do on a scene—— The hotel was planning to post them on to you, but they asked me to take them.' His eyes scrutinised her.

'How is Will?'

She jumped, nervous as a cat. 'Better, thank you.'

Still his eyes examined her face, too closely for comfort. She had the impression that he was waiting for her to say something more.

'What was the matter with him?' he said eventually.

'It was a virus of some sort. They still don't know quite what, but they had a couple of similar cases in at the same time.'

Brett still seemed to be watching, waiting.

Then he said. 'Elizabeth Garrett Anderson is a children's ward.'

Her eyes flew to his face.

Brett's expression was very set, very hard. He waited.

'Will is a child,' he said, finally. It wasn't a question, but a statement.

Her world, teetering on the brink of collapse for so long, finally fell around her.

'Yes.'

'Your child?'

'Yes.'

Beside her the taxi engine was throbbing, the meter ticking over. She put a hand against the door to steady herself. Brett's eyes raked over her so closely she thought they must read every thought in her head.

'How old is he?'

'He's—only young, very little.'

Brett pushed a hand through his hair. His eyes still held hers.

'What about his father?'

She forced herself to try and meet his eyes levelly. Somewhere, some time, she would have to tell him the truth, but this was the wrong moment in almost every way.

'He——' Janey paused. He watched her. 'Will and I live alone.'

Brett still held her look, almost visibly weighing her words, his face dark, assessing, stubborn.

Then with an explosive repressed oath he dashed back his cuff to check the time.

'I've got to go. I've got a plane to catch,' he said angrily.

She seized her moment. 'And I must get back to Will.'

Before he could stop her she jumped into the waiting taxi. Brett put his hand up to her window. 'I ought to warn you—Lynne Manners has done her worst. It's all in the *Herald* tomorrow.'

She received the news blankly. Everything was such a mess already, that one more problem hardly seemed to matter. She stared at Brett through the glass and he looked darkly back at her. Between them lay a tangled maze of emotions and misunderstandings, of hurt and anger, pain and puzzlement.

'Where to, miss?' the driver broke in.

She leaned forward to tell him and he pulled away, and Brett was gone.

CHAPTER ELEVEN

LIFE went on, apparently normally, but everything had changed. What had been solid ground beneath Janey's feet was now shifting sand.

She knew she was living on borrowed time, the final countdown before all her guilt and evasions finally exploded in her face.

First there was the diary item in the *Herald* that Brett had warned her of. It was the lead piece on the page, with prominent pictures of both herself and Brett. Under a picture of Brett striding, grim-jawed, towards an airport departure lounge was the caption 'Going . . .' Under a rather old picture of herself, taken at some Press reception or other, was the caption 'Staying . . .' The article was lengthy, but could, she reflected, realistically, have been far worse.

'At last some sketchy details of the private life of handsome, reclusive author Brett Britain have filtered out. Britain has long been known for his fear and loathing of publicity. Could it be something to do with a brief, failed marriage to Fleet Street's up-and-coming young notable, Janey Goodheart?

'It seems that both parties have kept their silence about their shared past. The marriage comes as news to even their closest friends. But Goodheart recently dipped her pen in poison to write a scathing profile of

Britain, and was shortly afterwards to be seen on the film set of his latest book, vociferously fending off all Britain's female admirers.

'What is going on? Is it hate, or love? Neither party is saying a word. Although dubbed the Flame-Haired Temptress, Goodheart is known on the social circuit only for her consistent refusal to join the party. Quiet domesticity is her after-hours preference. Britain meanwhile flew out to California yesterday, his only comment on the matter a phrase not fitting for a family newspaper.'

There was no mention of Will, and the worst details of the late-night scene between herself and Lynne Manners had obviously been kept quiet by the jilted actress.

Nevertheless, the piece prompted inevitable smirks and whispered comments as she walked through the news room that morning, and it was no surprise to find a note asking for her immediate presence in the Editor's office, on her desk.

'Well, Janey,' he said heavily, prodding a finger at the open copy of the *Herald* on his desk. 'What do you have to say about this?'

She opened her mouth, but no words would come. It was quite the worst moment of her professional life. She felt like a schoolgirl, found guilty of some stupid misdemeanour and about to be expelled.

'Is it true?'

'It's true we were—technically, are—married,' she acknowledged.

'I see.'

'I explained the situation to Tom,' she burst out. 'I

asked him not to send me, but he told me it was either go, or be fired. I——' Her mouth was dry. She swallowed. 'I obviously shouldn't have written the piece I did, but it was a very difficult situation. I don't want to go into private details, but there was a lot of provocation. I'm afraid the piece came out of blind anger.'

'I see,' he repeated. He sighed. 'What you did was very stupid, very unprofessional.'

'I know. It doesn't sound adequate, but I'm sorry——'

'You, and indeed, we, the newspaper, have got off very lightly. Mr Britain could have taken us to the cleaners if he wanted to pursue legal action. Of course, if Tom had been here, and not off in Australia, it might never have happened. He would have pulled the piece out like a shot—but he wasn't, and he didn't, and now we are all left looking very foolish.'

Janey looked down at the carpet. It was the same shade of green as Tom's, but it seemed half a lifetime since she had stared at his floor, through eyes swimming with the shock of being told she must see Brett again.

She had known it would be awful, but nothing in her wildest imaginings could have summoned up the tangled misery which now entrapped her.

'I could sack you for this, you know.' the words struck through her thoughts. She looked up, shocked to the core. She had to have her job to give Will the comfort and security he needed!

'However, I've decided not to,' the Editor continued. 'I can see you were under considerable stress, and I will assume nothing of the sort will happen again. But I have to warn you, Janey, this episode has put a question mark against your name for me. One mistake is permitted, but two are not. Keep your head in future—or you'll be losing your job.'

Lose her job! It was not something she dared contemplate. As the sole breadwinner, she had to pay the mortgage, meet the bills and supply all the treats she felt Will needed in his somewhat limited little life.

And these days the treats seemed more necessary than ever. As if responding to her worries, Will seemed to be changing, too. His horizons were widening and life in the tiny flat seemed too cramping for his growing energies.

She tried from time to time to begin preparing him to face the fact that he had a father, and a father whom she knew, would very soon be claiming all his rights. But Will would never sit still long enough to listen seriously to her, and if she tried to force him it quickly provoked a scene.

They were both tense and overstretched, just how much so she realised when, one Saturday, a string of tantrums had finally culminated in shouts and tears.

'We'll go to the zoo this afternoon,' she soothed him. 'We'll have a lovely time. You can go on the donkey cart, and have an ice-cream.'

But the outing was not the success Janey had hoped.

Will made enthusiastic faces at the monkeys and tried to scratch the rhinoceros's leathery back, but his interest soon flagged. She tried to maintain it with enthusiastic exclamations, but her own concentration was elsewhere, preoccupied with the haunting thought of Brett, and how she must tell him of Will's existence and her own deception over the years.

She had tried to draft a letter, to be sent, poste restante, to his publishers, but her writing skills had completely deserted her. Then she had thought about a telephone call to the States. But some deep instinct told her such news could only be imparted face-to-face, and she must simply wait, like a victim on an altar block, until he chose to get in touch again.

'Mummy, I want another ice cream.' Will's feet were dragging. She looked around. They seemed to be a sad couple in the midst of cheerful families. Other tired children, she noticed, were being swung aloft on to their fathers' shoulders.

'Come on,' she said, squeezing his drooping shoulder. 'We'll go home and maybe Simon will be there for you to play with.'

He brightened visibly, 'John said he would make us a tent in the garden,' he said. 'And he's going to teach us cricket.'

She felt her eyes prick with tears.

'That'll be lovely,' she said, masking the sadness in her voice. 'If we hurry we'll be back well before tea.'

But they made slow time on the crowded buses and tubes, and their progress down the road to the flat was at the pace of Will's tired feet.

So preoccupied was she with cajoling the little boy along that they were almost at the gate before she looked up. Standing on the pavement in front of the house, obviously awaiting her return, was Brett.

She gasped in shock. Will's head jerked up, turning dark, frightened eyes on her.

'What is it, Mummy?'

'Nothing, darling.'

Her heart was beating almost too fast to breathe. He had obviously been watching their laborious journey from the moment they had turned the corner. They were still thirty yards away, but with every step they took Will's features, his obvious parentage, would stand revealed.

Yet there was nothing in the world to do but keep walking. It was like journeying slowly towards a cliff edge, knowing that at some point there would be the inevitable sickening plunge.

The road was deserted. Brett's car was parked by the gate. He stood without moving, knowing she had seen him.

'What's that man doing?' Will registered the stranger at their door.

'He's come to see Mummy.'

She looked up. Now they were nearer, she could see Brett's eyes on Will, his expression unreadable. Closer still, and she could see a pulse of emotion beating at the angle of his jaw. They stopped. She looked up and met Brett's look, knowing guilt was written on her every feature.

'Brett—this is Will.'

Brett looked to the little boy and back to her. No words were needed.

'Will—this is a man that Mummy knows. His name is Brett.'

'Hello, Will.'

'Hello,' Will said reluctantly, his fingers tightening in her grasp. The air was thick with adult feelings that confused and frightened him.

Brett's eyes had been tugged back to the little boy.

Janey took a deep breath, her own fingers unconsciously tightening around Will's for support and reassurance. 'Let's go in,' she managed to say. 'Then you can go out into the garden, Will, and find Simon to play with.'

She led the way into her flat. Will ran off through the french windows just as soon as she released him, calling out to his friend in his exuberance at escaping from the electric atmosphere that filled the flat.

She watched him go, pausing before turning slowly back. Brett's thunderous figure filled her tiny living-room.

Neither spoke for a long moment. Then Brett said, slowly, 'Will Goodheart—or Will Britain?'

'Will Britain,' she said quietly, 'it must be obvious.'

Brett walked past her and stood watching the two little boys scampering between the fruit trees. For a long, long time he said nothing.

She sank into a chair. With the confession had come a curious lifting of her spirits, a lightening of the load. But she knew that the worst still lay ahead.

When he turned back, he said harshly, 'Why?'

'Why?' she repeated, stupidly.

'Why have I had a son for three years that I knew nothing about?'

'I didn't mean it to be like that——When I found I was pregnant I thought you would try and make me

have an abortion. Then later, I don't know——' To
her distress, dry sobs began to shake her. 'I was just
frightened. I thought you might try to take him from
me. Or——' she struggled to find words.

'Or?' Brett prompted, relentlessly.

'I couldn't imagine passing him backwards and
forwards like a parcel! There was no contact
between us. It seemed better it was like that——'
How could she tell him the ultimate truth? That to
have him in her life, as Brett's father, but not as her
husband and lover, would be a pain beyond
endurance?

'Can't you understand?' she pleaded. 'It wasn't
rational. It was an instinct—it was the only way I
could cope!'

He turned away from her, to seek out Will's
darting figure, as if turning away from ugliness to
beauty.

With his back to her he ground out, 'All I can
understand at the moment is that you've kept a son
from his father, and a father from his son! For three
years—no, three years and seven months if my maths
is correct—I've had a living, breathing, beautiful
boy that I've known nothing about——' There was a
note of true anguish under his anger. She heard it,
and the pain of it turned in her heart like a knife.

He turned back to her and said roughly, 'I've got
time to make up. Too much time. I want access, as
much as I need. And if you stop me, I'll fight you
through every court in the land!'

'You won't take him from me?' This time the
anguish was in her tone.

He laughed bitterly. 'Despite what you seem to think of me, I'm not in the habit of tearing babes from their mother's arms. I won't be kidnapping him, if that's what you're asking, and I've no intention of fighting for custody.'

'Then there will be no problems,' she heard herself saying.

There was silence in the room. She thought about the future. She was giving up Will, she knew, to a different future. But for him it would be better. Two loving parents instead of one. How she would learn to live with Brett's bitter anger and coldness she had no idea.

Brett was still sentinel at the window.

'Does he know about me?' he asked.

She shook her head. 'He's been too young to understand. I was going to tell him——I never intended not to. But the moment hasn't been right yet.'

'You'll tell him now.' It was a statement of command.

'Yes——' She thought. 'Brett?' There was a tone in her voice that made him turn.

'Yes.'

'Not now. Not this minute. He'll need time to get used to the idea. I couldn't just take you out and introduce you. Do you understand? I'm not putting it off. But I'll have to find a time when he's quiet and receptive, and then he'll need time for the idea to sink in.'

Brett nodded slowly, his eyes on hers. 'He's not the only one—although I've had more time, perhaps.

This is what I've suspected ever since I found out
Will was a mere child. It was the only thing that
made any sense. Except that——' he paused, his eyes
raking cruelly over her wretched face '—I found it
hard to believe that a truly loving mother could
behave like that.'

Janey flushed and looked quickly away.

He turned to watch his son again. When he spoke
his voice was odd and impersonal. 'I was supposed to
spend the next few months in the States, but I'll
cancel those plans now. This is my phone number.'
He scribbled on a piece of paper. 'When you think
Will is ready to spend some time with me, please call
me.'

He put the paper on a side table and stepped past
her, turning in the door.

'I will expect to hear within the next few days—if I
don't, I'll be round to see what has happened,' he
said, the threat clear in his voice.

She sat for a long time, not moving, as the boys
scampered to and fro outside. When she finally
called Will in, the light was going. She felt sick and
ashamed, frightened and relieved, all at the same
time, and she had no idea how Will was going to take
the news of his father.

But she need not have worried. After a long, soapy
bath and a carefully selected story which showed lots
of mothers and fathers going about their daily lives,
she found she was able to cuddle him close and tell
him quite easily that the man he had met this
afternoon was his father, whose work had taken him
away for a long time across the sea.

'Now he's back, he wants to come and see you and get to know you, and play with you and take you on outings.'

'With you,' Will said firmly, obviously unsure of this stranger in his life.

'We'll see,' she prevaricated. 'First of all I expect he'll just come and see you at home.'

'Will he live here?'

'No,' she said hastily, adding more gently, 'quite a lot of daddies don't live at home, do they? Like Joe's, at school.'

'His Mummy and Daddy are divorced,' said Will, proud of his new word, although obviously hazy about its meaning. 'Will you be divorced, too?'

'Yes, darling, I expect so,' she replied, squeezing shut her eyes to hide from him the expression of misery he might see there.

Dutifully she rang Brett and suggested he come to tea as soon as possible. It was not a success.

Will, responding to the strained atmosphere, clung to her and generally behaved as badly as he knew how.

Brett had bought a toy, not a flashy, expensive piece of bribery, she was glad to note, but a small intricate fire engine—just the kind of thing Will loved. Even so, he refused to go to Brett to have it demonstrated and came running after her the minute she got up to fetch something from the kitchen.

'Look, Will,' she finally said to him. 'I've got to go upstairs to give Ann a message. Why don't you take

Brett outside and show him how well you play football?'

Will opened his mouth to cry out in protest, but she pushed him firmly back into the room and escaped with a guilty sigh of relief at leaving the tense atmosphere behind.

Her excuse was a lie. The house upstairs was deserted, but from the living-room window she was able to watch discreetly, as slowly Brett managed to entice Will into a game. A hard knot seemed to slacken inside her chest. She thought it was fear for Will's sake, but she could not be sure it was not for Brett, as well, for both their feelings.

Certainly both players looked equally happy, and her heart ached at the apparent normality of the scene, because she knew it was not—would never be—a normal family life for any of them. Yet underlying it, too, was a strange equanimity. Life would be harder, much harder, for her now. She would have to loose the bonds she had bound round Will and let him go to his father, to develop new ties of love and trust. At the same time she would have to do regular battle with the love and longing for Brett that tore so savagely at her heart.

But she knew now that was better, far better, than the leaden burden of guilt that had dragged her down for so many long years.

CHAPTER TWELVE

FROM that moment in the garden Will never looked back. Brett managed to see him most days, and soon Will was happy to go off with him for quite long outings.

After a time he even began to talk excitedly about Brett's house in Scotland, and the boat he would learn to sail there.

Yet their own contact was limited to stilted doorstep exchanges, and brief words about Will's general health and welfare. She grew to dread the sound of his car in the street, the firm step down the path and the ring of the doorbell, and her urge to get the handover of Will finished with as quickly as possible made her curt to the point of rudeness.

In his turn Brett was brisk and cold, and had quite obviously not forgiven her for the way she had denied him his son's early years. No matter how much Will pleaded, he always firmly refused to stay for longer than was strictly necessary. And their eyes barely met over the little boy's head except in glancing, hostile exchanges.

She could not blame him, Janey thought, as she sat one Sunday afternoon in the strangely empty flat, leafing idly through an album of Will's baby and toddler years. She had denied him so much, from Will's first gummy smiles to his playgroup Christmas party. But his coldness towards her was like a knife in her flesh, and his regular visits were almost more than she could bear.

A sudden urgent peal of the bell made her jump up in alarm, the album flying off her lap. She flung the door open, Brett stood there, his face strained and anxious, his chest heaving. In his arms was a limp figure. Blood seemed to be splashed everywhere, in Will's hair and on Brett's shirt front.

'What happened?'

Brett pushed urgently past her into the flat and laid Will gently on the sofa. She ran to kneel beside the little figure, her eyes seeking the source of the blood. Will managed to smile through his tears as he saw her, and she put her arms about him, hugging him gently and muttering soothing words.

'He fell in the park,' Brett said. 'He was running towards the slide and he just tripped. He didn't seem to go down very hard, but he must have caught his head on a stone.'

'Can I see, darling?' With gentle, experienced fingers she began to part the matted hair. The wound was surprisingly small, less than an inch long and very shallow. As she explored his scalp, colour began to seep into his white cheeks and he struggled to sit up.

'Sssh!' She pushed him back. 'Lie still until I've cleaned you up. Then I think we'd better get the doctor to have a look at you, to make sure you're all right.'

She fetched water and antiseptic and began to sponge his hair and face. Brett sank down in a chair.

'What do you think?' he asked anxiously. 'Will he be all right?'

She looked closely at the wound again. 'I think so. It doesn't look too serious. And it's not in a particularly vulnerable spot. I don't think it's too bad. I think he was probably shocked, more than anything.'

Brett exhaled a long breath. She glanced across at the drawn, worried figure in the chair, his arms on his knees as he leant forward to study Will's face, and a fleeting grimace of sympathy crossed her face. She had lost count of the number of heart-stopping childhood accidents she had somehow survived.

She looked back at Will. 'I'm sure he's OK, but I think I'll ring the doctor, just to make sure he hasn't damaged his skull. Shall I ring you when he's——' Brett's look stopped her words. 'I'm sorry,' she whispered, 'that was stupid of me. Of course you want to stay.'

She got up and emptied the bowl of water and tucked Will round with a blanket before going to phone. Coming back, she almost collided with Brett in the hall. The flat seemed far too small for them all.

He raised bloodstained hands. 'Can I wash somewhere?'

'What——? Oh yes, the bathroom's there. If you take your shirt off I'll put it in the machine. It won't take long. The doctor said she would be half an hour.'

Slowly Brett undid his buttons, revealing the hard, muscled frame she knew so intimately. She turned away.

'Mummy, can I have a drink?' Will's voice

interrupted from the living-room.

'Best not to, until the doctor's been. Just to make sure. I'll only be a minute, then I'll come and read you a story.'

'*I'd* like a drink,' Brett said, bluntly. 'I thought he was half-dead—I need something to calm my nerves.'

'I've only got brandy, left over from making last year's Christmas cake. It isn't very nice.'

'As long as it's alcoholic.'

She fetched him a generous glass, then sat with Will, quietly reading his favourite book about a railway engine called Sam. Brett came back and sat sipping his drink and watching them both.

She sensed his observation, even though she could not directly see him. It made her deeply nervous, and she was relieved when the sound of turning pages signalled that he had turned his attention elsewhere.

The doctor, when she came, thankfully confirmed her diagnosis of no real harm done, but advised her to put Will straight to bed to sleep off the shock. Will for once made no protest but, as she leant to tuck him in, he muttered sleepily, 'I want Daddy to say goodnight, too.'

'He wants you,' she said, going back out.

Brett walked past her and she paused, watching him settle on the bed, his dark head bending close to Will's identical hair.

'Shall I tell you a story?' Brett said, and Will was soon lost in the intricate twists and turns of the plot.

The scene tugged at her heart. It looked so peaceful, so right—— But it was not right, not in any way. For her, having Brett in her tiny flat was like having a caged panther in her home.

She sat down. Left aside, on the chair, was the photograph album of Will's babyhood, open at his first birthday, and the sight flooded her again with memories and old hurts.

'Tell me about that, about all of it.'

Brett had reappeared noiselessly at her side. It was a command. He took the album and sat himself on the settee, peremptorily patting the seat beside him.

He opened the album at the beginning, at the pictures of her smiling wanly and apprehensively as she held an anonymous white bundle up to the camera. Beside her was her father, already gaunt from his illness.

Haltingly she began to talk, fumbling for words to describe those early months. Brett prompted her with perceptive questions. She described Will's first words, his crawlings, his determined attempts to walk. Slowly the words began to flow more readily. There was so much to tell, and she had never had anyone to share the joys and pleasures of her son. But Brett was broodingly silent when she finished. He got up, and went to the kitchen to replenish his drink.

Then he stood in the doorway, staring darkly at her. 'I've missed so much,' he said bitterly.

'I'm sorry—I don't know what to say—nothing can change the way things are——'

Behind them Will whimpered and turned in his sleep. They both looked round.

'Is he all right?' Brett looked anxiously to her for guidance. 'I'm still worried about his head.'

'I'm sure he's fine.'

'I should never have let it happen. I feel terrible about it. I was keeping an eye on him, but I thought he was safe just running.'

She sensed he needed reassurance.

'Look,' she said, 'it happens all the time with children. You just have to get used to it. They have a thousand accidents a year. You can't wrap them up in cotton wool.'

Although that was exactly what she had been trying to do, she reflected, before Brett came and broke through the protective shell that she, a single, anxious mother, was trying to build around him.

'You're a very good mother,' Brett acknowledged. 'Very calm and loving. You've done a good job.'

The unexpected compliment ran like honey through her veins, making her blush with pleasure.

'I'm not,' she said quickly. 'I've made millions of mistakes. It's just that Will's a lovely boy. I——' She struggled for words. 'I was wrong to think I could bring him up alone. He really needs you, I can see that now. His life has been quite different recently. He needs a man in his life.'

There was a long silence.

'What about you?' Brett said, in a low voice. 'Don't you need a man, too?'

She looked up. The tension in the room seemed to rise around them, the atmosphere charged, electric. Brett stepped towards her, drawing her up. His thumbs stroked the soft skin of her arms, making her shiver under his touch. 'You've got needs, too, Janey. They might not be to play football, or talk about fire engines, but they're every bit as real——'

'Don't! Leave me alone.' She managed to drag her arms from his hands, even though the light caresses of his fingers made her tremble inside.

She crossed the room, but he was behind her, his hands on her shoulders.

'Perhaps it's my turn to apologise,' he said. 'I said things about you I know now weren't true. I thought you—— Well, you know what I thought. I assumed Will was your lover, at least at first. Later on I didn't know what to think.'

'No one's my lover,' she said tightly, forcefully. She had only loved once, and look what heartache and pain that had brought! She was finished with that! Will and her work would be enough.

Brett's hands pulled her back closer to him. 'That doesn't seem right. You're not made to live like a nun.' His hands slid from her shoulders, down the curves of her arms and waist, a deliberate, provocative caress. Then his fingers slipped round her waist, and his lips sought her neck, her ear, with teasing kisses deliberately arousing her until her senses whirled.

She tried to think of Will, asleep next door. It all seemed wrong. Their brute, colliding passion had no place here.

'Don't,' she said again, pulling her head away, 'it's not right.' It wasn't. Blind passion, devoid of love— her body craved him, but her mind rejected the heartbreak it must bring. A visiting father was one thing, but a father who stopped to make casual love to the mother on his way out was quite another.

'Why not?' Brett turned her in his arms, his voice tight. 'Don't you understand? I can hardly bear it. Just seeing you on the doorstep, then having the door shut in my face. When what I want to do is hold you, touch you, kiss you——'

He kissed her on the mouth, ravagingly, before she could stop him, his mouth opening hers, and his arms pulling her closer, moulding her softness.

She wanted it, too. Or her body did, yielding to his with the same instant desire he had always aroused. Beneath her palms was the strength of his back, those firm muscles. Such an illusion of strength to lean against! She had to resist it. Brett offered her nothing at all except the quick explosive fireworks of physical contact.

His lips roamed her neck, her shoulders. His hands found her breasts, which stiffened to his touch with a life of their own. Shudders of pleasure reached down to her furthest depths.

Brett said he could not bear to stand on her doorstep and not to reach out for her. But she could not bear it when he reached out and then left. He would have had what he needed, but for her the real ache of longing would only just be starting.

She tried to think these thoughts as Brett kissed her, but his own need was rousing all too full a response in her. He groaned a muffled sound as he pulled her still closer to him, his hard body pressing the length of her. 'Janey, how I've wanted you.' Now his hands were at her waist, beneath her loose T-shirt, moving up to seek her breasts again. 'For heaven's sake, let's get rid of these clothes.'

Holding her close he led her to her bedroom and laid her on the bed. Then he kissed her again, pulling off her T-shirt and kissing her bare skin until she was as fevered as himself. She was ashamed of her need, ashamed he could do so readily whatever he wanted with her. As he stood back to pull off his own shirt, his eyes taking in her slim figure, half-naked on the bed, she turned her head away. Her eyes were squeezed shut. Tears were forming, and she could not stop them. One welled through her lashes and ran down her cheek, then another, and another. She curled on to her side, knees up, seeking the ancient foetal position of comfort.

Sobs were following the tears now. She forced them back, but they still made the bones of her ribs shake and her shoulders heave.

Brett froze.

'Janey!' he cried in alarm, and sat down, a hand trying to still her shaking shoulder.

His voice was a final trigger. Suddenly the tears were a flood, the sobs racking, wretched, gulping cries that, once started, she could not stem.

She was crying because the very thing she had most dreaded had happened. Brett had walked in and disrupted her life as only he knew how to do. She was helpless in his power, victim of her uncontainable longing for him. She had been strong, but now she was weak again, devoid of will, of the power to say no.

But now she was crying for everything else as well, all the loneliness and pain of bringing Will into the world alone, the death of her father, the long, hard struggle to build a life for themselves in London.

She was crying because she hadn't cried for so long, not for years, not fully and helplessly, because she had denied herself self-pity, and now she was flooded with it, because she had been wrong, so very wrong, to hide Will's birth from Brett, and because of Brett, and how she loved him, and would never have that love returned.

'Janey, what is it?' Brett's hands held her. She could feel his eyes, dark, on her face. She pressed it further down into the pillow, bringing her knees up tighter. No one could help her, especially not Brett who was the very source and fountain of all her pain.

He said nothing until her storm of sobbing slowly began to abate. As it did he raised her to him, holding her in his arms, rocking her like a baby, stroking and soothing her as no one had done for years. She kept her eyes closed and allowed herself to be comforted, even though part of her knew it was an empty illusion.

'Tell me,' he urged her, his voice low but insistent. She shook her head, the gasps of her dying sobs still shaking her frame. She hid her head. She did not want him to see her like this, tear-stained and weak.

'You must.'

'I can't!'

'Why not?'

'You—— You wouldn't understand.'

'Try me.'

'I just want you to go away.'

Brett turned her head to face him, his eyes going over her face.

'Do you? Do you really, Janey? Tell me the truth.'
She could no longer hide from his gaze.

'I know what you're thinking!' she cried. 'Well, you're right! I still want you. I always have wanted you. I've never been able to hide it. You could easily make love to me now, any time, if you wanted to! You've only got to touch me, kiss me, and I'm a—what's the word?—a push-over! But it isn't enough! I can't live like that! Don't you see?'

His hands gripped her arms as he looked into her eyes. He said nothing. She felt driven to go on.

'That's why I didn't tell you about Will. One of the reasons. I knew I wouldn't be able to cope if you were around, especially if you still wanted——'
She faltered.

'To take you to bed,' he prompted. 'Make love to you. Which I do.'

'It's easier for men. They can just do that and walk away.'

'Which is what you did to me, exactly what you did—it wasn't me that slammed the door on our marriage, it was you.'

'But you were pleased! I know you were! We both knew it couldn't work——'

'I knew it was a mistake at the time,' he acknowledged. 'Neither of us knew how to handle the commitment. I told myself that I wanted to do the right thing by you, and that's why I suggested marriage, but I suspect my motives were far more mixed. I knew you were special, and I wanted to capture you, to make sure no one else got hold of you. But I should have let you stay free, allowed you to go without any guilt, so you could grow up at your own pace, and in your own time.'

'Well, I'm grown up now,' said Janey bitterly. 'Grown up enough to know that having a good time in bed isn't the way to find happiness.' She managed to extract herself from his grasp and walk away. Then she said tensely, 'Please leave me alone, Brett. When you come to see Will, please don't try and resurrect our relationship. I can tell you now that if you do, you'll always succeed. But it's not what I want, and it's not the best thing for Will, either.'

'Why not?' His question was harsh, abrupt.

'Will needs me to be strong, in control. It's how he expects me to be. You make me weak and unhappy——'

'Perhaps you've been in control for too long, Janey.'

'What do you mean?'

'I can understand why it's happened, but it looks to me as if you're in danger of becoming too hard, too isolated from other people. You can forget how to have friendships, you know, forget how to love——'

Tears started again in her eyes. She hugged her arms round herself. How could he say that of her? Forget how to love! She had never forgotten, that was the whole problem!

'I don't see how being your casual mistress could solve those problems,' she flung out, her voice shaking from held-back sobs. 'Your sexual lure isn't a remedy for all ills, you know!'

There was a long silence behind her. She did not hear him cross the room to her, but he was suddenly behind her, hands on her shoulders, turning her round to face him. His hands were gentle and his voice low. 'Who said anything about casual——'

Her eyes rose to meet his.

'Don't you understand? I've never been able to put you out of my mind, Janey, not since the day I first saw you. We shouldn't have married, not because it was the wrong thing, but because it was the wrong time. You were scarcely more than a child, and I was too overwhelmed by my own sudden success to think clearly about anything.

'After you left me I longed to come chasing after you, to bring you back, but I knew how unhappy I'd make you, so I forced myself to leave you alone. I told myself if you really wanted me you would come back to me in your own time, when you felt ready.'

Her eyes widened. 'I thought you didn't care——'

'I tried not to. I went here, there, everywhere. I worked like a trooper and tried to get involved in other relationships, but nothing worked. Scarcely a day went by when I didn't think of you, and coming back to London was always agony. I would see your name in the *Standard* and wonder what had happened to you since we were together, what your life was like. I wanted to telephone you, but something always stopped me. Pride, I suppose, and fear. I dreaded hearing that you were living with someone else, that you wanted a divorce.'

She shook her head, her eyes still on his, their purple depths open in wonder at what she was hearing.

'There's never been anyone else. No one at all. I've

never wanted anyone else.'

'Because of Will?'

'No, not just that. At first I just felt wretched. I wanted you so much, but I thought I'd made such a fool of myself that you would never want to set eyes on me again. Then there never seemed to be time to think about anything at all. My father needed so much nursing, and I was so worried about being pregnant and coping with a baby——When I finally came to London there were offers, of course, but never ones that interested me. I think something inside me died the day I ran away from your flat, and didn't revive until I saw you in Scotland——'

He crooked a smile at her. 'Why do you think I insisted it was you that came? I didn't want to do any damn interview—but it seemed a perfect chance to engineer a meeting, without any loss of face on either side if it proved a disaster.'

She could not tear her eyes from his. 'I knew the minute I set eyes on you that nothing had changed between us,' he went on, 'but there was so much tension in the air—I thought at first it was just a straightforward matter of sex. I thought if we could get that out of the way we would have some chance of talking to each other like civilised human beings. That's why I tried to force the pace. But then I realised there was something else, something I didn't understand. You seemed so defensive, so aggressively determined to lash out at me.'

'I didn't mean to hurt you, I was just so terrified of seeing you again, not knowing why you'd summoned me like that. And there was Will——'

'I thought my worst fears were realised when I first heard his name,' he acknowledged. 'And when you told me on the way down to Dorset that he wasn't ever going to be thrust aside, there was something in your tone that made me realise that if he was my rival I might as well throw in the towel there and then.'

'Oh . . .' She remembered their lunch, the sudden lightening of tension. 'I couldn't understand why your mood seemed to change so suddenly. It was a relief in a way—but I couldn't bear it when you went off with Lynne Manners.'

He grinned. 'I didn't exactly—perhaps I'm a better actor than she is! I was rather hoping to make you jealous, although the end result was far more dramatic than I could have predicted!'

He paused, letting his eyes take in her every feature. Slowly his hands moved to frame her face. When he spoke again his voice was very quiet, very serious. 'When I asked you to come to Mull I wanted to see if we'd grown apart or together over the years. I knew the answer to that the minute I set eyes on you again. I can't forget you, Janey. I can't walk out of here now and leave you alone, like you asked. You fascinate and entrance and infuriate me. I love your impulsiveness, that curious mixture of strength and weakness, sophistication and shyness. I suppose I'm saying I love you——'

Her lips softened and parted in disbelief at the wonderful words.

'But what about Will? What I did——'

'It hurts,' he admitted, honestly, but his hands still

cupped her face. 'I wanted to do terrible things to you when you first told me. I still feel furious when I think of all the time I've missed——'

'I hate myself for what I did,' she burst in. 'It was so selfish! All I was thinking about was my own fears and feelings, and how hard it would be for me to have to see you all the time when I still loved you so much—I didn't really think about you or Will at all!'

'Oh, my darling,' he said softly and his hands slid round her back to gather her close to him. 'We've both got a lot to forgive each other for. I've said some dreadful things to you in my jealous rages. If we're to give each other a chance we'll have to wipe the slate clean and start from scratch. I can do it, if you can.'

'I think I could forgive you anything,' she said. 'I love you so much, I always have done. Right from that very first moment. I knew then what I felt, and I knew it would never change.'

Slowly he embraced her, kissing her fully and without restraint. It was an embrace of love, not anger—slow and sweet and sensuous. She let herself sink into his arms, holding him for the first time with all the gentle care and love she felt for him. Time was forgotten, and so was urgent passion. Now, at last, there was time not to hurry, time to go cautiously and make mistakes and mend them again.

Brett said, 'What can I say? I want to ask you to marry me, but you're already my wife.'

She pulled back slightly, needing to say something urgently to him.

'Brett, I'm still scared. We've made so many mistakes. We need time—you, me and Will.'

'We've got it,' he assured her. 'All the time in the world. I'm not letting you go again, either of you. We're a family now, and we're staying together, come what may.'

Once more his lips sank to hers.

'There's only one thing,' he said, raising his head.

'What?' Her eyes opened to his, shadowed with apprehension.

'I've never liked the idea of only children. And there are all those empty bedrooms in Mull.'

'Oh!' She smiled in loving relief at such a simple problem. 'I'm sure we can do something about that—if we try!'

Harlequin *Presents*

Coming Next Month

1079 DARK DESIRING Jacqui Baird
Believing her trip to Sicily with her boss is for business, Helen finds
herself trapped. Carlo Manzitti, the Italian who captured Helen's heart
two years before, and from whom she had fled, has arranged the whole
thing. This time he intends to keep her.

1080 THE POSITIVE APPROACH Emma Darcy
Ben arrives in Sarah's life like a rescuing knight, with a solution to both
their problems. He needs a wife; Sarah needs a fresh start. He says he'll
make all her dreams come true—but eventually Sarah begins to want
more than just dreams....

1081 ECHO OF PASSION Charlotte Lamb
Zoe, hurt by Rory Ormond before, is determined to prevent the same
thing happening to another young girl. She believes she's over their affair
and strong enough to thwart Rory's plans without danger to her own
emotions. Until she meets Rory again.

1082 LOVESCENES Sandra Marton
Shannon angrily voices her opinion on music celebrities who walk into
jobs for which real actors would give their eye teeth. Unfortunately,
Cade Morgan hears her—and can't resist the challenge. That's how it all
starts....

1083 WISH FOR THE MOON Carole Mortimer
Lise Morrison was an innocent trusting girl until her love for Quinn Taylor
shattered her world. But Elizabeth Farnham is less vulnerable, now, more
sophisticated. She can cope with anything...except perhaps the
reappearance of Quinn.

1084 TIME OUT OF MIND Kay Thorpe
Adria Morris, suffering from amnesia, is startled when Kyle Hamilton
appears and proves she is his late brother's wife. Even after her return to
their family home on St. Amelia, her amnesia persists. Adria must decide
whether to marry Kyle, or leave behind all hope of regaining her memory.

1085 LOST LAGOON Anne Weale
Interior designer Alexandra, headed for the top, isn't going to be swayed
from her career, even by someone as special as Laurier Tait. And Laurier
isn't the type to settle for a brief autumn affair—he wants a full-time
partner in life.

1086 THE ORTIGA MARRIAGE Patricia Wilson
Meriel has made a life of her own since her stepbrother, Ramon Ortiga,
rejected her love. Now, because of her young half brother, Manuel, she
returns to the remote Venezuelan ranch to find Ramon as arrogant as
ever—and her attraction to him still as strong.

Available in June wherever paperback books are sold, or through
Harlequin Reader Service:

In the U.S.
901 Fuhrmann Blvd.
P.O. Box 1397
Buffalo, N.Y. 14240-1397

In Canada
P.O. Box 603
Fort Erie, Ontario
L2A 5X3

HARLEQUIN *Temptation*

Give in to Temptation! Harlequin Temptation

The story of a woman who knows her own mind, her own heart . . . and of the man who touches her, body and soul.

Intimate, sexy stories of today's woman—her troubles, her triumphs, her tears, her laughter.

And her ultimate commitment to love.

Four new titles each month—get 'em while they're hot. Available wherever paperbacks are sold.   Temp-1

Penny Jordan

Stronger than Yearning

He was the man of her dreams!

The same dark hair, the same mocking eyes; it was as if the Regency rake of the portrait, the seducer of Jenna's dream, had come to life. Jenna, believing the last of the Deverils dead, was determined to buy the great old Yorkshire Hall—to claim it for her daughter, Lucy, and put to rest some of the painful memories of Lucy's birth. She had no way of knowing that a direct descendant of the black sheep Deveril even existed—or that James Allingham and his own powerful yearnings would disrupt her plan entirely.

Penny Jordan's first Harlequin Signature Edition *Love's Choices* was an outstanding success. Penny Jordan has written more than 40 best-selling titles—more than 4 million copies sold.

Now, be sure to buy her latest bestseller, *Stronger Than Yearning*. Available wherever paperbacks are sold—in June.